"It doesn't have to be complicated. You and me and a mutual attraction. It doesn't come much simpler than that."

"Good times—is that all you're about?" Ellie shook her head. "Of course you are. Men like you always are."

"Men like me?"

"Arrogant, ego as wide as the blue Aussie sky. Always looking out for number one."

Matt studied her. The telltale blush, the sparkle in those eyes, the way her fingers played over the back of the chair. "You're a contradiction, do you realize that? You say you don't want complicated, yet you're rejecting simple. What *do* you want, Ellie Rose?"

Her mouth tightened and she swept to the door, yanked it open. Then she turned and glared back at him. "With you, Matt McGregor? Nothing. I just want to be left alone."

D0833071

When not teaching or writing, **ANNE OLIVER** loves nothing more than escaping into a book. She keeps a box of tissues handy—her favorite stories are intense, passionate, against-all-odds romances. Eight years ago she began creating her own characters in paranormal and time-travel adventures, before turning to contemporary romance. Other interests include quilting, astronomy, all things Scottish and eating anything she doesn't have to cook. Sharing her characters' journeys with readers all over the world is a privilege…and a dream come true. The winner of Australia's Romantic Book of the Year Award for short category in both 2007 and 2008, Anne lives in Adelaide, South Australia, and has two adult children. Visit her website at www.anne-oliver.com. She loves to hear from readers. Email her at anne@anne-oliver.com.

WHEN HE WAS BAD...

ANNE OLIVER

~ MAVERICK MILLIONAIRES ~

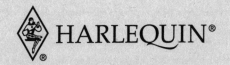

HARLEQUIN®

TORONTO • NEW YORK • LONDON
AMSTERDAM • PARIS • SYDNEY • HAMBURG
STOCKHOLM • ATHENS • TOKYO • MILAN • MADRID
PRAGUE • WARSAW • BUDAPEST • AUCKLAND

If you purchased this book without a cover you should be aware
that this book is stolen property. It was reported as "unsold and
destroyed" to the publisher, and neither the author nor the
publisher has received any payment for this "stripped book."

Recycling programs
for this product may
not exist in your area.

ISBN-13: 978-0-373-52803-5

WHEN HE WAS BAD...

First North American Publication 2011

Copyright © 2010 by Anne Oliver

All rights reserved. Except for use in any review, the reproduction or
utilization of this work in whole or in part in any form by any electronic,
mechanical or other means, now known or hereafter invented, including
xerography, photocopying and recording, or in any information storage
or retrieval system, is forbidden without the written permission of the
publisher, Harlequin Enterprises Limited, 225 Duncan Mill Road,
Don Mills, Ontario, Canada M3B 3K9.

This is a work of fiction. Names, characters, places and incidents are
either the product of the author's imagination or are used fictitiously,
and any resemblance to actual persons, living or dead, business
establishments, events or locales is entirely coincidental.

This edition published by arrangement with Harlequin Books S.A.

For questions and comments about the quality of this book
please contact us at Customer_eCare@Harlequin.ca.

® and TM are trademarks of the publisher. Trademarks indicated with
® are registered in the United States Patent and Trademark Office, the
Canadian Trade Marks Office and in other countries.

www.eHarlequin.com

Printed in U.S.A.

WHEN HE WAS BAD...

CHAPTER ONE

'IMAGINE him naked.'

Ellie Rose barely heard her friend's voice above the night-club's musical din, but she recognised the lusty tone. She knew why. And she knew to whom she was referring. The six-foot-something male-model type standing not more than fifteen feet away. As the gyrating crowd parted briefly beneath the swirl of dimly coloured neon lights and bone-jarring bass, she was treated to her first full-length glimpse of him.

He was turned away from her, but she could see that he was tall and dark and… She had a thing for cute rear ends. One butt cheek tightened and… Nice, she thought with a little sigh that tickled like a guilty pleasure down to her toes. Very nice.

Then the crowd closed around him and she cursed her height-challenged five foot two. But no way was she admitting to ogling him with the same lustful thoughts her friend had voiced. She hadn't known Sasha long, but she did know that she was more than likely to up and invite him over. From what Ellie had observed, Sasha didn't wait for men to find her; she found them.

Ellie feigned ignorance. 'Who?'

Sasha lifted her bottle of wine cooler in salute and raised her voice over the noise. 'You know perfectly well who—the guy up close with that tall chick in leather pants. Better still, imagine yourself naked *with* him.'

Ellie could. Very well. Too well. On indigo satin sheets... Except that the stunning brunette leaning in for a kiss insisted on sabotaging the image. Ellie swallowed and said in a ridiculously tight voice, 'We're not here to pick up guys. We're here to enjoy the music.'

'Speak for yourself.' Sasha tipped her bottle to her lips. 'If you want to enjoy music, go see a musical. Uh-oh, I think he's looking at us,' she said. 'At you,' she amended as the crowd between them thinned. She pressed her knuckles into Ellie's spine, prodded her forward. 'He's coming this way. Go on. You could get lucky tonight.' Sasha leaned closer, spoke into Ellie's ear. 'Ask him if he's got any friends.'

Ellie's legs began to tremble. She didn't want to get lucky. Did she? No. Not with a guy who had the potential to make her want things she knew she couldn't have with a guy like him. He had *permanent playboy* written all over that cocky smile and confident stride.

He wore black trousers and a white open-necked shirt that reflected the ceiling's changing light show. His hair was dark, short and spiked with a touch of gel in such a way that it looked as if he'd just rolled out of his lover's bed. The designer platinum watch adorning his wrist screamed money, money, money.

The lighting changed to an intermittent strobe—it seemed to flash in time to her pulse—as he drew near. And then he was so close that a quick yank of her arm would bring him within lip-smacking distance, and it was like watching one of those flickering black-and-white movies.

His eyes were dark bottomless pools. Mesmerising, magnetic, reeling her in. 'Hi, there. Can I buy you a drink?'

His voice, liqueur over dark chocolate, slid down deep, coating her insides with its lusciousness. She raised her all-but-empty bottle of cola. 'I already have one, thanks, and I'm with a friend…' She trailed off as she saw Sasha making off into the knot of dancers, hips swaying. The rat. This little dinghy was doomed.

'Looks like your friend knows how to have a good time,' he said, his gaze following Ellie's briefly before turning back to her. 'I haven't seen you here before.'

'Because I haven't been here before. I'm not a regular clubber.' Sasha had dragged her along despite her protests, insisting Ellie needed more fun in her life.

'Let's make you one.' He reached for her hand. 'Dance with me.' A tingling sensation zipped all the way up her arm and settled low in her abdomen. His hand was warm, hard, firm. The way she imagined the rest of his body would feel. She recalled her sheet fantasy—and the brunette. Tension gripped tight in her lower belly.

'What about your friend?' She slipped her hand from his. Smoothed the tingly palm over her little black dress. Hitched her miniscule embroidered bag higher on her shoulder.

Uh-oh. Big mistake, voicing that observation, because now he knew she'd been checking him out. But he couldn't know what she'd been thinking…

Or perhaps he did, because he grinned—the way a man like him *would* grin if he knew—and Ellie wished she'd never given him the satisfaction.

'Yasmine's a colleague,' he said, that sexy confident grin still in place. 'I haven't seen her for a while. I've been working in Sydney.'

Hence, the up close and personal, Ellie supposed. She darted a quick glance behind him. She saw a well-endowed blonde in a white halter neck watching him with avaricious intent, but she could no longer see Yasmine. Or maybe her name wasn't Yasmine at all; maybe she'd just given this guy the flick and he'd moved on to his next target—Ellie. She didn't know him; he could be lying, looking for an easy lay.

And when it came right down to it, who here wasn't?

She wasn't.

Her body wanted, desperately, to refute that claim—*with him*—but she injected the zap of excess hormonal energy into her spine instead, straightened and stuck to something inanely neutral. 'You're from Melbourne originally?'

He nodded. 'I work on multiple projects, so I commute between the two cities on occasion.'

And he obviously took the high road to town, whereas she lived on the low road.

'The name's Matt, by the way.'

No surname, Ellie noted. Obviously not interested in more than a passing flirtation. Fine. Long-term relationships and becoming attached to people always ended in disaster. At least, it did for her. She lifted the bottle to her lips and drained the contents to soothe her throat which felt as if it were coated in sand. 'I'm Ellie.'

'How about that dance, then, Ellie?'

A ribbon of heat shimmied through her as the music changed to a slow, thrumming love song.

Body contact.

Perspiration broke out between her breasts, on her upper lip. She tugged at the neckline of her dress a couple of times to create a draught. It didn't help. 'I'd rather not at the moment, if you don't mind…' Except that the bosomy blonde was sure to pounce…and Ellie found herself smiling up at him. 'It's so airless and loud in here, I—'

'Outside, then?' he suggested. 'I could do with some fresh air myself.'

Even better, Matt thought as, with a light hand at her back, he guided her around the sway of dancers toward the club's secured outdoor area. The sensation of skin-warmed fabric was a tantalising heat against his palm. Anticipation—a different kind of heat—nipped at his skin.

But she stopped midstride and swivelled to face him, looking for all the world like a bunny frozen in headlights, and for a moment there he thought she'd changed her mind. He was prepared to do whatever it took to change it back again, but she gestured to the cloakroom.

'I…I'll want my jacket. It might be hot in here, but it's bitterly cold outside.'

He watched her walk towards the cloak check. He hadn't intended picking up a woman tonight. He'd come to get away from the pressures of work for an hour or two, but the petite woman with the short flyaway bob had captivated him. Perhaps it was because she was nothing like the women he usually dated.

He liked his women the way he designed his million-dollar constructions—tall, clean-cut lines, elegant sophistication and a sense of style. This girl was tiny, delicately boned but curvaceous. Moreover, every curve looked real. She reminded him of fairy floss—pretty and sweet and fragile.

That warm nip of anticipation struck anew. Harder, hotter. He ran a finger around the collar of his shirt. His suggestion to step outside had been inspired because suddenly he couldn't wait to find out if she tasted as sweet as she looked. And then…then he wanted to take his time to enjoy, something not easily achieved on a crowded dance floor.

He watched her hand over her ticket to the attendant, her spiky stilettos drawing attention to the smooth, well-turned ankles, her short hem riding up her thighs as she reached over the countertop to collect her coat.

'Hi,' a sultry feminine voice said beside him. 'I couldn't help noticing your friend leaving.'

He barely glanced at the woman who'd materialised beside

him. Blonde. Big…teeth. 'She's not leaving,' he said, his gaze finding Ellie again.

Ellie turned and wide wary eyes met his. She looked away, then looked back, nibbling on her lower lip, and for the second time in as many moments he thought she might bolt to the exit.

To forestall that possibility, he stepped forward quickly to meet her, cupping her elbow as he drew her towards the outdoor area. 'Everything okay?'

'Why wouldn't it be?'

'You looked a little edgy for a moment there.'

'Did I?' A tentative sound between a laugh and a cough escaped her as she accompanied him outside.

An almost solid wall of cold air laden with cigarette smoke met them. Bright lanterns swung overhead, reflecting pools of colour on aluminium tables and overflowing ashtrays. Clubbers huddled in groups around tall gas heaters, smoking, drinking and laughing while couples smooched in shadowy spots around the high-fenced perimeter. And by an amazing stroke of luck one of those spots appeared to be reserved for them.

'This is better.' He took her jacket from her hands—a little black number with embroidery on the pockets—and settled it around her shoulders. Her bobbed hair, cut just below chin length, brushed silkily against his fingers.

Her fragrance teased his nostrils. Not perfume, but something that smelled like spiced raspberries. 'Now we can talk without risk to our vocal chords.' Her eyes intrigued him. Beneath their placid reserve he glimpsed the promise of passion. 'So, Ellie, if you're not into the club scene, what do you do for fun on a regular Saturday night?'

'I read. Science fiction and fantasy mostly.' Shrugging deeper beneath her jacket, she said, 'I know…that probably sounds pathetically solitary and boring to someone like yourself.' She rolled her eyes to the star-studded sky. 'But haven't you ever wondered what's out there?'

'Sure.' He shifted his gaze—not skyward but to the tempting column of her throat. 'For now, though, I'm perfectly satisfied with what's right here in front of me.'

'Oh…'

He blinked. *Oh? That was it?* Most women would respond with a smile or a giggle or a flutter of lashes—some hint that this game was definitely going somewhere.

Not Ellie. And yet there was no mistaking the latent heat behind her gaze. She tugged the edges of her jacket together with tightly curled fingers and switched topics. 'What's been happening in Sydney?'

He rocked back on his heels. 'To tell you the truth, I've been too busy to notice.'

'Doing what?'

'I'm working on a harbour-side housing project at the moment. How about you? What line of work are you in?'

She moved her shoulders. 'A bit of this, a bit of that. I like to move around, so I pick up work wherever.'

'Travel. So I'm guessing you've been overseas?'

She coughed out a laugh. 'I'm afraid nothing near as exciting as that. Name a town between Sydney and Adelaide and I've probably been there at some stage in the past few years. I don't like to be tied down.' She laughed again but the humour didn't seem to reach her eyes. 'Call me irresponsible.'

'Okay, but at some point, you'd probably like to settle in one place, build a career and take on the responsibility of raising a family?'

She shook her head once. 'Not me. I'm a free spirit. I go where I please, when I please. And I like it that way.'

Do you? he wondered, watching the play of mixed emotions flicker across her gaze.

'And I can eat the whole darn cheesecake in one sitting

if I want. Now that's what I call freedom.' Her smile broadened. This time her eyes danced with devilment and he found himself totally entranced by the way her lips curved, making apples of her cheeks.

'I guess it is,' he agreed, smiling back. 'Free spirit, huh.' His lips tingled in anticipation of his first taste of her luscious-looking lips. He could almost feel their sweet heat, the warmth of her breath against his cheek.... 'Ellie, I want to kiss you,' he murmured. 'I've been wanting to kiss you since the moment I laid eyes on you.' And a lot more besides, but he didn't voice that yet.

Her head snapped back, her eyes locked on his and the slow-burning sexual tension which had been simmering along nicely evaporated in a puff of frosty air. Her tongue darted out to lick her lips, then they disappeared altogether as she pressed them into a tight flat line.

His body howled a protest. *That's what you get for being a gentleman, McGregor.* He'd not had much experience with women knocking him back. Or he was right and she wasn't as *free* spirited as she was making out. 'Is there someone else?'

'No.' Her face reflected the light from the pink lantern hanging nearby as she shook her head.

'So...?'

Nearby, someone's glass shattered on the concrete but her eyes remained locked with his. They seemed to say yes, but her behaviour indicated otherwise. The wind scuttled along the high brick fence, scattering dried leaves at their feet and riffling through her bright hair, gleaming like moonlight.

Then her shoulders tightened as she drew in air. 'So...do it, then.'

Her surprisingly breathy demand had his libido leaping to attention. He leaned closer, watching her chest rise sharply as she drew another swift breath, watching her eyes flare with a mix of vulnerability, hesitance and anticipation.

He barely laid his lips on hers, just enough to feel the warmth there, the texture. It was like tasting summer's first ripe peach. Sweet, soft. Sensuous. Eliciting a low throaty murmur from her that sang like honey through his bloodstream.

More. It was more than he'd anticipated and it threw him for a loop. He lifted his head to gaze down at her, saw that she was as surprised as he. He hadn't expected to feel his heart beating oddly out of time, as if he stood on the top of the Sydney Harbour Bridge in the middle of a storm without a safety harness.

Willing to believe it had been a fluke, again he lowered his lips, felt her hesitance dissipate like autumn mist in sunshine as she shifted nearer. Her mouth, tentative and unsure, softened and opened beneath his. He took swift advantage, lifting his hands to cradle her jaw for more intimate access and angling his body so that they aligned in the all right places.

He felt her tiny frame quiver against him as he swept his tongue inside her mouth to tangle with hers where the flavours were richer, darker, hotter.

Ah, *now* she didn't resist. In any way. She was right there with him—he knew by the way her tongue curled with his, the way her body turned fluid and malleable against him. He stepped closer, her legs tangling against his.

Either she didn't notice or she didn't care. Her hands slid up the front of his shirt. He could feel his heart pounding into her flattened palms. Then she slid them down again and wrapped them around his waist, and leaned in so her breasts pushed against his chest.

He let his hands wander too, over the smooth creamy column of her neck, the delicate heart pendant she wore, inside her jacket until they found the neckline of her dress. Down, palms skimming the outside of her breasts, the womanly shape where her waistline dipped, then flared again as he traced her hips. She was perfection. He wanted more. And with the way she was melting against him, it would appear he was in luck.

Ellie's knees were so loose it was a minor miracle she didn't collapse right there on the pavers. Her pulse thundered, her blood sizzled. Her only thought was she couldn't believe that she was letting this man—this *god*like man who smelled sinfully good and probably did this every night of the week with a different woman—kiss her to kingdom come.

Then her eyes closed, her mind shut down and all she felt was sensation. His hands warm and firm on her body, his unfamiliar hot, potent flavour, the sound of fabric shifting against fabric as he drew her closer.

And she was clutching his shirt without even realising she'd reached for him. Her body was burning without any recollection of who'd lit the fire.

His hands began a more intimate journey, seeking out her hardening nipples, drawing them into stiff peaks against the bodice of her dress. Rolling them between finger and thumb. She gasped as wetness accumulated between her thighs and, like a wanton, thrust her breasts forward, willing, *willing* him to keep doing what he was doing.

He did. Oh, yes, he did. But the ache only intensified, his clever hands sending ripples of desire straight to all her secret places. Her belly rubbed against a powerful ridge of masculinity. A moan rose up her throat at the sensation of the contrasting hardness against her softness.

A ragged answering groan seemed to come from the depths of his being. 'How far to your place?' he murmured thickly against her neck.

His voice and the message conveyed broke the lust trance she'd been momentarily lost in and her eyes snapped open. The harsh streetlight over the wall haloed his head, leaving his features obscured. All she was aware of was a dark silhouette looming over her and the unfamiliar scent of a man she really didn't know at all.

Oh. My. God. Panic clawed up her throat and she pulled free. 'I…I need to go to the ladies'.' Clutching her jacket about her shoulders, she took a couple of steps away, and from the safety of distance she pulled her thrumming lips into some semblance of a smile and said, 'I'll be back in a moment.'

She plunged back into the overheated room, saw Sasha amongst the dancers and caught her eye. Sasha winked over some guy's shoulder and twirled her index finger in the air— their prearranged 'goodnight' signal should they decide to leave separately.

Ellie nodded, manoeuvred her way through the dancers, past security at the entrance and out onto the street, still busy with traffic despite the late hour.

A car filled with loudmouthed teenagers cruised past, their car stereo's bass competing in an out-of-sync rhythm with the club's. Cold air stung her face and bare arms as she clung to her jacket, desperately willing a taxi to appear.

'Wait, Ellie.' She jumped at the sound of his voice behind her, but she didn't turn around.

No, no, no. If she looked, she might reconsider and she couldn't risk that. A fleeting kiss was fine, a little flirting… probably. But a kiss like *that*, with a man like *him*… A man who could sweep away her common sense without raising a sweat…

A frantic wave brought a taxi screeching to a halt in front of her. She dived inside, slammed the door and ordered the cabbie to *drive*.

But before he could pull into the stream of traffic, the door swung open again. Her breath caught and her fingers tightened on top of her bag. Matt whoever-he-was filled the space with his unique brand of woodsy midnight cologne, his smile, his charisma. 'You dropped your jacket,' he said, and laid it on the seat beside her. He didn't attempt to climb in.

'Ah… Thank you.' She hadn't even realised it had slipped off her shoulders and felt like a fool. He hadn't done anything she hadn't wanted him to and she'd taken the coward's way out and ditched him without one word of explanation. Worse, she could see the blonde who'd eyed him up earlier watching the proceedings from the club's entrance.

'You sure you don't want to change your mind?'

No. She dragged her eyes back to his. 'Yes.'

'"Yes," you're sure, or "yes," you want to change your mind?'

She shook her head. 'You know what I mean.'

His smile faded. 'Maybe, but I'm not sure you do.' He withdrew a wallet from his hip pocket, flipped it open and pulled out a black-and-gold business card. 'When you do… change your mind…'

When I do? That's why she stayed away from men like him. They messed with your head; they were dangerous… and addictive. And when they were finished with you, what did you have? Emptiness, pain and regrets.

When she didn't take the card, he reached inside and grasped her hand with his large warm fingers, turned it palm up. He pressed a kiss to the centre, then replaced his lips with the card, folded her fingers over the top. 'Until I see you again.' Spoken with all the arrogance and confidence in the whole damn universe.

Her palm burned and she curled her fingers into a fist. *Protecting the imprint of his mouth or screwing up his card?* 'I don't think so.'

But he just grinned, as cocky as ever. He peeled off a one-hundred-dollar note from his wad. 'Cab fare home. Pleasant dreams, Ellie.'

* * *

Ellie unlocked the door to her one-room studio apartment, stepped into calming darkness and solitude, grateful none of the other tenants she shared the building with were around to witness her dishevelled state.

Leaning back against the door, she let out a sigh. She could hear her own breathing, still ragged, her pulse, still rapid. What had she been thinking? Letting him kiss her and then… *oh*…and then letting him come on to her that way? And what was she supposed to do with all that change from the cab fare?

Closing her eyes didn't help. It didn't block the images or shut out the memory of how she'd responded to him. 'Idiot!' she snarled. 'I am an idiot.' She recited the words slowly through clenched teeth. Her fingers closed tightly over the business card she still held. She hadn't been able to make herself drop it in the gutter like she should have.

Crossing the room, she tossed the crumpled cardboard on her night stand *without* looking at it, flicked on her bed-side lamp and flung herself onto her narrow bed, pulling her comforting pink rug over her body. Then, just to be sure, she sent Sasha a text telling her she'd gone home. Alone—in case Sasha got smart and sent her a fun text about 'getting lucky'. *Lucky?* She stared at the ceiling as if she could read answers in the ancient water stains.

She didn't want to get lucky. She didn't want to get involved. With anyone. Not that Matt had come even close to suggesting any such thing. It had been obvious where his intentions had been focused. But a late supper, maybe a few dates and who knew where that would have led? On her part, at least. *You know exactly where,* the little voice in her head whispered.

She didn't know how, but Matt was unlike any man she'd ever met, and that made him dangerous. Didn't mean she didn't know his type. He'd probably already forgotten her.

She'd always been one to get easily attached to people. And

when they left, for whatever reason, they took another piece of her with them.

Like when her part-time father walked out on her and Mum for the final time. She'd been three. Then three years later there'd been the car accident which had taken her mum and both grandparents. Her father had come back into her life to take care of her, but he was and always had been a wanderer. It had been a glorious adventure, travelling with him around the country chasing work, but she'd been a hindrance, and at the age of nine he'd left again, tearing out her young heart, and she'd found herself in foster care.

As she'd grown up she'd had boyfriends, and two and a half years ago her first and only serious relationship.... She shook her head against the pillow. No, she wasn't going to think about Heath. But the memories slinked back anyway, like wolves waiting to pounce.

They'd been inseparable for six months. Ellie had thought Heath was serious, but no... Instead, it seemed the gorgeous Brit she'd fallen for had an expiring work visa and the not-so-little complication of a fiancée waiting for him back in London. He'd told her it had been great while it lasted but she'd been a fling, didn't she understand that?

Her hands clenched around the sheets. Matt whoever-he-was hadn't only ignited a fire in her belly; one look into his eyes, one brush of his lips over hers and she'd forgotten everything she'd taught herself about self-preservation.

No. Those days were *over*. She'd never allow herself to get close to a man again. To fall in love. And most definitely, absolutely, she'd never risk marriage and kids. Matt was wrong about that. So wrong. 'No, Matt whoever-the-hell-you-are,' she said to the ceiling. 'I will not change my mind.'

CHAPTER TWO

ON TUESDAY morning, after he'd seen Belle safely off at the airport, Matt headed upstairs. Belle's century-old six-bedroom Melbournian mansion was maintained in spotless condition, but she'd left his old bedroom alone and a good clean-out was well overdue. He planned to slot it in between appointments he'd arranged at the city office over the next few days.

He'd get started while waiting for this mysterious employee—Eloise someone—to put in an appearance tomorrow.

Eloise. The name reminded him of Ellie, which brought back memories of Saturday night. He'd thought he had it made. Until she'd pulled her disappearing act. He'd spent the rest of the night in acute discomfort and his body still hadn't quite recovered. A week or so of mutual enjoyment would have filled the evenings here very nicely. He dismissed the fact that he could have enjoyed a few hours with Belinda the busty blonde and frowned as he reached the top of the stairs. It had been Ellie he'd wanted.

He knew the interest had been reciprocated. The eternal question would always be why she'd changed her mind. Obviously she had some hang-up that she hadn't deemed fit to enlighten him about.

Still, for a few moments there in the shadows, gazing

into those captivating amethyst eyes, he'd been completely charmed.

He shook the memory away. Right now he had a more immediate concern. Until Belle had phoned last week, he'd never heard her mention anyone by the name of Eloise. And seeing that look in Belle's eyes today when he'd waved her off on this impulsive trip—visiting Miriam, some woman she'd not seen in fifty-odd years in North Queensland—was a real concern.

'Miriam's the sister of a man I once knew,' she'd told him when she'd rung to see if he could house-sit while she was away—something else she'd never done.

'After all these years, why now, Belle?' he'd asked.

'Because something's happened and I need to make a decision and she's the only one who can help me make it. I'm sorry, Matthew, I can't tell you more. Not yet.

'There's something else,' she'd continued. 'A new employee you haven't met will be working there while I'm away. Her name's Eloise and I want you to look out for her.'

He'd agreed. Of course he'd agreed.

Then this morning... 'Don't forget, I need you to be nice to Eloise,' she'd reminded him as he'd escorted her to the departure gate.

'I'm always nice.'

For once, Belle didn't smile. 'Matthew, this is not a frivolous matter.'

Belle was the closest person to a mother that he had, and he'd known her for more than twenty-five years, but he'd never seen this particular expression in her eyes before. Fear? Desperation? Hope?

He frowned. 'If you're worried about leaving her unsupervised, why can't you just tell her to come back when you return?'

'She needs the work. Moreover, I'm afraid she might leave.'

'If she needs the work, she won't leave.'

'I don't want to take that chance. She—' Biting off her words, she smoothed a finger over his furrowed brow. 'And don't scare her off with that stern all-business facade.'

'I am in business, remember?' Which always made him wary of others' motivations. 'What's so special about this particular employee?'

Her short caramel-coloured hair was permanently tamed to within an inch of its life but Belle ran a restless hand through it. 'It's complicated. That's why I need to take this trip. To talk to Miriam, to consider and then to make a decision. And I need you here to keep an eye on…everything.' She wrapped her fingers around his forearm. 'Promise me, Matthew.'

'Of course, Belle, you know I will.'

She presented her boarding pass to the attendant. 'I know you have questions and I appreciate you not pushing me for answers.' She reached up, kissed his cheek. 'Thank you for coming. I think you'll like Eloise—you might even become friends. She'll be there tomorrow. You might take her out,' she suggested. 'Get to know her better…'

He felt his eyebrows lift. *Friends? Take her out and get to know her better?* Was that *hope* in Belle's voice? She'd never been a matchmaker, so there was something else she wasn't telling him. He returned the kiss absently. 'Why the urgency, Belle? Come back with me, let's meet this Eloise person together and we can discuss whatever it is that's worrying you.'

But she shook her head again and moved into the stream of passengers heading for the air bridge. 'A few days, Matthew. I'll explain everything when I come back.…'

She'd told him that *she'd* phone *him* when she was ready. At least he'd made her promise to text him that she'd arrived safely. Still pondering his concerns and whether he should intervene in some way, he pushed open the door to the familiar bedroom.

Cartons he'd never got around to sorting were crammed against one wall. Age had faded the once-bright carpet square. Grime from storms past dulled the mullioned windows.

But nothing could dull the memories of waking up in this room to sunlight streaming through the glass and spilling rainbows across his *Star Wars* quilt. To the aroma of hot toast and bacon. Belle had always insisted on a good breakfast.

Unlike his biological mother, who'd not even bothered to stick around, nicking off in the middle of the night and leaving no more than a note saying she was sorry. *Sorry?*

Zena Johnson, single mum—and pole-dancer on her evenings off, it had turned out—had been Belle's housekeeper until she'd skipped town, leaving her only son with her employer. The best decision Zena had ever made, for all concerned, Matt reminded himself, without a lick of regret for the woman who'd given him life.

Belle had taken that scared, lonely, introverted kid, who'd never formed attachments since they'd never been in one place long enough, and treated him as her own. Loved him as her own. To Matt, Belle was family, and fourteen years ago at the age of eighteen he'd taken her surname to prove it.

He hefted the first carton, overloaded with his old school books. Time for the recycling bin. But the box was flimsy and slid out of his grip, spilling the contents over his feet. Dust billowed over his sneakers and jeans, then rose to clog his nostrils. He swiped a dust-coated forearm over his brow. Okay, the job might take longer than he'd anticipated—

A flash of movement somewhere beyond the window caught his eye. He saw a female figure walking up the leaf-littered path. Frowning, he moved nearer, rubbing a circle on the glass with the hem of his T-shirt for a better look. Not walking, he noted now—more like bouncing, as if she had springs attached to the soles of her worn sneakers. Or a song running through her head.

Young—late teens, early twenties? Hard to tell. He couldn't see her face, shadowed by a battered black baseball cap, nor her hair, which she'd tucked out of sight. She wore a baby-pink T-shirt under baggy khaki overalls with stains at the knees. What looked like an old army surplus backpack covered with multicoloured daisy graffiti swung from one slender shoulder.

She slowed and, with her face in shadow, uncapped the bottled water in her free hand and stood a moment, staring at the old unicorn statue in the middle of the lawn. Something about her tugged at the edges of his mind.

He tracked her progress along the carefully tended topiary and gnome garden statues. How had she slipped past the gate's security code? She wasn't the first trespasser on Belle's property—the reason he'd had the damn thing installed for her in the first place.

Only one way… She'd climbed the fence.

Every hair on his body bristled. Young, agile, probably doe-eyed and short on cash—she was just the sort to take advantage of a trusting woman living alone.

Not this time, honey.

He crossed the room, descended the stairs, half expecting the front doorbell to ring. He yanked open the door but saw no sign of her.

Where the hell had she gone?

He hotfooted it through the kitchen, his sneakers squeaking over the tiles, and shoved through the back door. Scouring the grounds, he spotted her slipping inside the old garden shed, partially obscured by ivy at the far end of the estate.

Heading grimly across lawn damp from last night's rain, he barely noticed the stiff autumn breeze whistle through his threadbare T-shirt. But he noticed the scent she'd left on the air. Subtle and clean and...somehow familiar...

Barely visible in the shed's gloom and with her back to him, she was inspecting gardening tools, discarding some, dumping others in the wheelbarrow beside her, all the while humming some unfamiliar tune slightly off-key.

He stopped at the open doorway, leaned an arm on the doorjamb. What was her game plan? he wondered, watching her add a pair of gardening gloves to her stash.

She couldn't be more than five foot two and what he could see of her was finely boned. She didn't look dangerous or devious, but he knew all too well that looks were deceiving. A gold-digger in overalls? Something niggled at him and he waited impatiently for her to turn around....

Ellie knew she wasn't alone when the light spilling through the doorway dulled. A tingle swept across the back of her neck, cementing her to the spot. The tune she'd been humming stuck in her throat. The fact that whoever it was hadn't spoken told her it wasn't Belle.

And he was blocking her only escape route. Her mouth dried, her heart rate doubled. Trebled. The stranger was male. She could feel the power and authority radiating off him in waves. And something else. Disapproval. Red-hot disapproval, if the heat it generated down her spine was any indication. Was he a cop? She tried to recall if she'd jaywalked on her way here but her brain wasn't computing anything as simple as short-term memory.

A cop wouldn't sneak up on her.

She could smell sweat and dust.... Barely moving, she closed the fingers of her right hand around the handle of the gardening fork which, by a stroke of luck, already lay in the wheelbarrow beside her hip.

Heart jumping, she grabbed the fork with both hands and

swivelled to face him at the same time. 'That's close enough.' Her voice grazed the roof of her mouth like the dry leaves at her feet. To compensate, she jutted her chin, aimed the fork in the direction of his belly and hoped he hadn't noticed the tremor in her hands.

In the windowless shed all she could see was his silhouette. Tall, dark. Broad-shouldered. One bulging arm holding up the doorframe. Why hadn't she flicked on the light as she came in? She aimed the fork lower, straight at his crotch. 'I'm not afraid to use this.'

'I don't imagine you are.'

There was something familiar about that deep, dark voice which made her stupid heart jump some more, but in an entirely different way. More of a skip.

She jabbed the fork in his direction. 'You're trespassing. Miss McGregor'll be coming out at any moment.' At least, Ellie hoped she would…or maybe not, since Ellie would be forced to defend the woman as well as herself. 'She's probably already ringing the police.'

'I don't think so.' His voice, frost-coated steel, sent a chill down Ellie's spine.

'Back off. Now.' Heart thumping hard again, she lunged forward, rotating the fork's tines to a vertical position so that they lay a dangerous whisker away from his jeans. From this position he towered over her and it belatedly occurred to Ellie that all he had to do was open his hand and her weapon would be his.

But he didn't attempt to confiscate it, nor did he step back. As if he knew she couldn't carry through with her threat, and there was nothing overtly menacing or desperate in his demeanour when he said, 'How did you get in and what are you doing here?'

'I used the code Miss McGregor gave me. Did you think I scaled that seven-foot fence?' She shook her head, realising that was probably what he thought. 'I'm the gardener—who are you?'

'You're Belle's gardener?'

She drew herself up at the barely veiled sarcasm. 'That's what I said.'

'What happened to Bob Sheldon?'

'He still comes in to do the heavy stuff.'

This man knew Belle's name and was obviously familiar with her staff. Still... Ellie's fingers relaxed some on the fork. Her arms ached with holding the thing but she didn't lower it. Not yet. 'You haven't told me who *you* are.'

Then he stepped back, into the sunlight, and said, 'Matt McGregor.'

Brown eyes met hers. *Familiar* brown eyes. Eyes she'd dreamed about for the past couple of nights.

Her entire body went into lockdown. *Oh, no. Not him. Please, please, please. Her Saturday night almost-lover couldn't be Belle's nephew. Couldn't be.*

'What are *you* doing here?' Her words came out on a wheeze.

A tiny twitch in his right cheek was the only sign that he recognised her. Her fingers slid off the fork as he took it from her boneless grasp and let it drop to the ground beside him. 'I might ask you the same question, *Ellie.* Or should I call you Eloise?'

'I already told you, I work here. And only Belle calls me Eloise and gets away with it.' Forcing herself to meet his gaze, she squinted up at him from beneath the bill of her cap. Same eyes—without the heat. Same beautiful mouth. The same mouth that had kissed her crazy. A tremor rippled down her body, her nipples puckered in loving memory.

That mouth wasn't smiling now.

'I'm here to keep an eye on things in Belle's absence.'

By sheer force of will, she drew herself up and attempted

casual. 'Belle's gone already? I thought she was leaving tomorrow.'

'She left at six this morning. As you'd have discovered if you'd knocked at the house first.'

She glared up at him. So *this* was Belle's hot-shot architect nephew with the million-dollar business—which she'd have known if she'd only looked at his card. What were the odds? She should buy a lottery ticket.

'Belle sometimes sleeps late,' she informed him coolly. 'I like to start early. I usually greet her when she comes outside with her morning coffee. I'm running late today because—'

'You had to wash your hair?'

How did he know? Her hand rose automatically to her cap and she sighed. 'Several times, actually.' But it hadn't made much of a difference. It was still pink.

'Ellie.' The sound of her name rolled out like a boulder over a grassy knoll. 'Ellie…what?'

She straightened her spine. 'Ellie Rose.'

'As in hyphenated?'

'As in Rose is my surname. My mum's surname, actually,' she explained. 'My father didn't want a kid so Mum…' She trailed off. *Too much information, Ellie.*

'Well, Ellie Rose,' he said, still eyeing her as if she might pick up the fork the moment he turned his back. And, by crikey, she was tempted. 'If you'd come up to the house…'

A sense of foreboding slid through her. 'Pardon? Belle doesn't—'

'Belle's not here. *I'm* asking you.' He inclined his head. 'Please.'

'Is this because I didn't come to work last Friday? I went on a field trip to the botanic gardens and I thought I'd make it up today, so that's why I'm a day earlier.'

'Just come with me,' he said, gesturing towards the house, and she realised her tongue had run away from her. Again.

Stress, that's what it was, but trying to explain would only make it worse. Was it because she'd left him on Saturday night without any explanation?

He was already walking away, his lanky stride putting more distance between them every second. Ellie couldn't help it; she couldn't drag her eyes away from those tight jeans clenched around that familiar butt. Temptation on legs.

No, she told herself and darted back into the shed to grab her backpack. Never again. Gorgeous overbearing men were *not* her type.

Lose the attitude, Ellie. You need the work. Focus on the *work.* Swinging her pack over her shoulder, she hurried to catch up, the nervous fingers of her left hand twirling around the button on her overalls strap. And wouldn't you know it—the pesky thing came away in her hand. The bill of her cap bumped into him, knocking it off and sending the brass disc spinning over the grass in front of him. 'Oops,' she mumbled to his back. His very broad, very hard back.

He spun around, firm hands closing around her upper arms. She barely had time to absorb their heat and the long lean feel of them before he let her go.

'My button... Sorry,' she muttered again, and while she was rubbing away the tingles his touch had wrought, he was bending over and searching for her button in the grass. She watched the muscles flex and roll on either side of that long curve of spine, the enticing sliver of bronze flesh below his T-shirt. She wondered what he'd do if she just reached out now and ran her fingernail across—

He straightened abruptly as if he knew exactly what she'd been thinking. She cleared her throat, attempted a smile and held out her hand. 'Thanks.'

He didn't smile back or answer. He was too busy staring at her hair.

And she'd been too busy checking out his butt—his

back—to pick up her cap. She swiped it up, aware that her cheeks probably matched her hair by now. 'Supermarket brands… Never mind.' She jammed her cap back on. She was never, *ever* going to put a colour through her hair again.

'Fairy floss,' he murmured to himself, still eyeing her cap as if he could see through it.

He dropped the button into her outstretched palm before turning and continuing to the back door, leaving her to struggle with the strap as she followed. She slipped its end through the bib's buttonhole and tied it into a temporary knot and prayed it held.

The kitchen smelled of lemons, cinnamon and rosemary. A homey room with sparkling red and white china and a friendly collection of ceramic cows on the pine dresser. The fragrant miniature potted herbs on the windowsill had been a gift to Belle from Ellie.

'Have a seat.' He pulled out a chair at the table for her.

Their knees bumped as he sat and his eyes flicked to hers, as if he, too, had felt that zing of sensation. She shifted her legs out of harm's way. Wringing her hands beneath the tabletop, she chewed on her lip to stop herself speaking before he got started on whatever he had in mind.

He set his hands, palms down, in front of him on the table and considered them carefully before he looked at her. 'I have some questions.'

About Saturday night? Why she'd changed her mind? Rushed off? Not called him?

No. His eyes weren't asking those questions. This was more like a job interview. It didn't seem to matter to him that Belle had already hired her. 'I thought Belle would've told you about me.'

While she spoke he pulled out a fancy-looking black and silver electronic organiser and began tapping. 'Not enough,

I'm afraid.' His finger paused over the buttons. 'First up, how did you come by this job?'

'Belle contacted me through an ad I posted in the local paper. And she hired me on the spot because I'm a damn good gardener,' she finished, leaning back and crossing her arms. 'That was a month ago, and it must be true because I'm still here.'

He didn't reply, just continued to study her with a steady, impenetrable gaze. Not a hint of Saturday night's heat there. Ellie refused to be disappointed. Refused.

Maybe if she explained why he could trust her to do a good job... Leaning forward again, she said, 'This house holds a special significance for me. When I was a kid my mum and I used to walk past here on the way to the tram. She told me the property had been in my grandfather's family at one time. The house was a little girl's fantasy and I loved it—especially the unicorn statue in the front garden. Its horn used to be gold, you know.'

His gaze turned considering. 'I know.' He studied her in silence a moment longer, then tapped his fingers on the table. 'References?'

'I've moved around a lot.' *Call me irresponsible.* Her words spoken in part jest, part bravado last Saturday night spun back to haunt her. Racking her brain, she tried to recall what else she'd said, but unfortunately could think of nothing that would instil confidence.

'Ah, of course, the free spirit.'

She watched those long fingers punch more buttons while heat bled up her neck and her nipples tingled. Those fingers had—

'No references. Your address and phone number?'

Her gaze whipped up to his face. That tiny muscle twitched in his jaw again but his eyes betrayed nothing. Not a thing. The heat continued to rise, suffusing her cheeks. She twisted restless fingers around the locket at her neck. 'Look, I really don't see that this is any of your concern. I'm Belle's employee, not yours.'

'Belle can be a little too naive sometimes. I'm making sure she's taken care of. Address? Phone number?'

'Belle has them.'

'She's incommunicado. What if something comes up? I need to be able to contact you.'

Holding his gaze defiantly, she snapped out the information.

'What days do you work?'

'Wednesdays and Fridays and I alternate Mondays and Tuesdays, but—'

'I value responsibility. Belle values responsibility. You call yourself irresponsible. So I'm wondering where that leaves us. Or more to the point, where it leaves you. I'd like you to think about that while you're working here.' He leaned back in his chair and placed his hands on the table. *Interview over.*

Thank goodness his unfathomable dark eyes didn't drop below her face. Thank goodness her chest was hidden beneath her overalls, because no way her skinny T-shirt would have been enough to hide the sudden way her nipples begged for more of that attention he'd given so generously Saturday night.

But then the cool business facade disappeared. His eyes thawed to a warm chocolate, lips curving into that lazy smile she'd seen across a crowded nightclub. 'Now we've got that out of the way,' he said in that deep sexy tone she'd been fantasising about in her daydreams. 'Have dinner with me tonight.'

CHAPTER THREE

DINNER? She stared at him, incredulous. He looked genuinely serious. 'Excuse me? You expect me to go to dinner with you?'

'Why not?'

'After that…that *inquisition*?'

'You need to understand my first concern is for Belle. But we've discussed the terms of your work here. I'm satisfied—' plucking a violet from the little vase in the centre of the table, he twirled it between his fingers '—with the business aspect of our relationship.' He flashed her a look that had her heart rate picking up again.

'But we haven't talked about the personal. We need to. If we don't, it's going to get in the way.' He leaned towards her, tucked the violet behind her ear, just beneath the edge of her cap. 'Never mix business with pleasure, Ellie.'

Her insides rearranged themselves at the intimate tone of voice. She didn't want business *or* pleasure with this man.

Liar. Okay, it wasn't wise or sensible to have anything more to do with him—certainly not pleasure. Already *un*-sensible thoughts were racing through her head.

Which reminded her of Belle's comment over a coffee break one day. *Matthew's always been a bit of a playboy when it comes to the ladies*, or some such. Ellie hadn't taken much notice—until now. Well, she did not intend to play second fiddle to anyone, ever again.

'I'm thinking I'll give this job a miss until Belle returns,' she said slowly. She placed her hands flat on the table and forced herself to meet his eyes. 'It's probably best for everyone concerned.' Particularly Ellie. 'I don't think the employee-employer relationship bit's going to work for us.'

His jaw firmed; his gaze turned thoughtful, then speculative. 'In which case, there'd be no reason not to have dinner with me, would there?'

She shook her head. 'I still can't have dinner with you.'

'If you're worried about your hair…mishap, we can dine in.'

Oh, way to charm the girls, Mr Ladies' Man.

She tugged the bill of her cap lower, tossed him a narrow-eyed glare and didn't deign to reply.

Or maybe it was just her. She bet he wouldn't say *that* to the type of high-maintenance, *high-class* Yasmine look-alikes he probably dated. He'd told her he was in Melbourne for a couple of weeks. Saturday night proved he was simply out for a good time, and if she hadn't left when she did they'd have ended up in bed. And that would have been a monumental mistake.

Pleasure had definitely been on Matt's agenda, but if that wasn't going to happen, so be it; he intended keeping his promise to Belle. Somehow he needed to keep Ellie happy in her job and ensure she stayed on. And what better way than to keep her close, keep an eye on her? Smiling at her, he switched to his most persuasive tone. 'Ellie, it's just dinner. I'd like your company this evening.'

Unmoved, she met his gaze squarely. Her eyes were the most amazing colour—amethyst with a sprinkle of gold dust… Bewitching…

Focus, McGregor. 'Okay, you may as well know up front. Belle asked me to look out for her employee while she's away. I'd like to be able to tell her I've done so.'

A tiny frown furrowed between her brows. 'I don't need looking after. Why would she ask that of you?'

Wouldn't we both like to know? 'Seems she's grown very fond of you and was concerned about you working at the house alone. Since I was going to be around, it seemed like a good solution.'

She waved a dismissive hand. 'It's all irrelevant because I have to work tonight. At least Red's Bar doesn't give their employees the third degree. I was hired on the spot, no questions asked.'

'Red's Bar.' Surely they'd eat a girl like her alive? 'That's not a reputable bar and it's not in a safe part of town.'

'*Some* of us can't be choosy. *Some* of us need cold hard cash to pursue our dreams.'

He didn't bother telling her he'd been there, done that and had the scars and papers to prove it. 'And what's your dream, Ellie?'

'To build my own landscaping business. Oh, and did I tell you I'm studying landscape and garden design? In modules. When I can afford it. At the rate I'm going I should be qualified in the next fifty years or so. Which is why I need Red's pay packet at the end of the evening.'

Landscaping business. He nodded to himself. Good, honest work. But what job did she hold at Red's? he wondered, eyeing the defiant lift to her chin. Kitchen hand, bartender, waitress? Or pole-dancer, like his long-lost mother? The thought made him feel physically ill, with a whole bunch of complicated emotions he didn't want to think about whenever his mother came to mind.

But the stubborn image that gyrated before his eyes had

his blood plummeting below his belt. If Ellie chose to pole-dance, he wanted it to be for him. In private.

Back on track. He cleared his throat and chose the safest option. 'Waiting tables?'

'Yes, *waiting tables*, what else would it be? Oh…' A rosy pink bloomed on her cheeks—those apple cheeks that had blown him away the first time he'd met her. When he'd just had to kiss her…

Ignoring his body's response, he focused on the valid reason he was still pursuing this line of questioning. She was playing in an adult playground—did she know the rules and, more importantly, the dangers? But perhaps she was already an experienced player. After all, he hardly knew her.

He knew he wanted her.

Her heightened colour intensified. 'What?'

'How long have you worked there?'

She lifted her shoulders, avoided his eyes.

'How long?' he demanded.

'It's a trial shift.' She pushed up. For once she had the height advantage and her eyes met his, bright with defiance. 'And your *babysitting* duties do not extend to telling me where I should or should not engage in paid employment. Now, if you'll excuse me, I have a kitchen garden to be getting on with. Since I'm already here, I'll work out today's shift.'

She pushed the chair beneath the table with a sharp scrape. 'And in case you're wondering, I use the outside loo, I brought my own packed lunch and can let myself out the gate when I'm through for the day. I'm sure you have work too. Lots of work. So if you want to go to the office and catch up with Yasmine…or whatever, don't let me spoil your day.'

Sparks, he noted. Promising. Where there were sparks there was emotion. Passion. Possibilities. He felt a smile kick up at the corners of his mouth. 'My day's going just fine, thank you.' Even better when he saw her fingers tighten around the back of the chair as she glared at him.

'Before I leave, there's still the matter of what went on between us Saturday night,' he said, unable to resist looking at her lips one more time. 'As I said, ignoring it won't change things.'

She sucked in a breath, studied her hands. 'It was just a kiss....'

A snort escaped him. 'Hey, I was there, remember?'

'Okay, it was more than a kiss.' Cheeks blazing, she lifted her gaze. 'It was a *mistake*. You're Belle's nephew, Belle's my employer and—'

'So you *are* going to reconsider working here.'

She shook her head and continued. 'I don't want, nor do I have time for, anything complicated.'

'It doesn't have to be complicated. You and me and a mutual attraction. It doesn't come much simpler than that.'

'Good times—is that all you're about?' She shook her head again. 'Of course you are. Men like you always are.'

'Men like me?'

'Attractive, arrogant, ego as wide as the blue Aussie sky.'

He studied her. The *you-don't-fool-me-for-a-moment-McGregor* stance, the nervous way her fingers played over the back of the chair. 'You're a contradiction, do you realise that? You say you don't want complicated, yet you're rejecting simple. What *do* you want, Ellie?'

Her mouth flattened and she swept to the door, yanked it open. Then she turned and glared back at him from the safety of distance. 'With you, Matt McGregor? Nothing. Not a thing.'

Uptight young lady, he mused. Damned if he wasn't going to enjoy finding out why. 'You know, Ellie Rose, I'm going to prove you wrong about that, and believe me, it's going to be a pleasure.'

He grinned as the door shut firmly behind her. 'Yes, a real pleasure,' he murmured. 'For both of us.' He was in for an interesting week.

Matt rode the glass elevator to the Melbourne offices of McGregor Architectural Designs, watching a rain shower draw a grey curtain across the cityscape. He never failed to feel the thrill of the ride up to his office on the forty-second floor. The award-winning precinct of glass and brass and green, with its unique interior-walled gardens cascading over half a dozen floors down towards a pool in the main lobby, was his first major achievement. Proof that one could turn possibilities into something real.

And his rapidly expanding Sydney branch was proof that success bred success. He'd worked bloody hard for it. In a roundabout way he had Angela to thank. His ex-lover was the reason his was one of the top architectural firms in Australia. After she'd given up trying to make something of their relationship and eventually walked out on him, he'd put his heart and soul into building his dreams.

Not that he blamed her for leaving. She deserved better than a guy who was incapable of the everlasting love and long-term commitment she'd obviously been looking for. And no-one could tell him he wasn't pleased to know she'd found it with an accountant in rural Victoria.

The current Sydney project was nearing completion. He trusted his hand-picked team of specialist engineers to handle it for a couple of weeks, enabling Matt to think about relocating back to Melbourne in the near future. The city he'd been raised in. Home.

The elevator slid to a soundless stop and he stepped out. Light spilled through the floor-to-ceiling windows and over miles of pearl-grey carpeting and polished wood.

Joanie Markham, the first face the public saw, glanced up

from the sleek polished reception desk as he approached, her middle-aged smile sparkling at him over her slim reading glasses.

'Good morning, Joanie.'

'Mr McGregor, good morning. We weren't expecting to see you today. Didn't Miss McGregor have something she wanted you to take care of?'

An image of Ellie shot into his mind with the force of a blowtorch. And not the image he *should* be focusing on—Ellie in cap and sexless khaki overalls wielding a gardening fork. Instead, he saw Ellie *not* in her little black dress and toothpick heels. He could almost taste that soft skin just below her jaw, her spiced berry scent....

She was something to be 'taking care of', all right. He pinched the bridge of his nose, concentrated on bringing his wayward libido under control.

'Mr McGregor...are you okay?'

'Fine. Fine.' Amazed that his eyes had closed—not surprising with the lack of sleep he'd had over the past few nights— he blinked them open and pasted a reassuring smile on his lips. 'All under control, Joanie.'

Moving past reception, he skirted desks, design boards, pot plants, greeting staff along the way.

'Matt.'

He turned at the familiar sound of Yasmine's voice. As usual, she looked stunning in a slim grey suit with a modest scrap of white lace at her cleavage, her raven-black hair tied back in a tidy knot. He admired her clean-cut lines from an architectural viewpoint.

As a friend, he valued her inner qualities. 'Hi, Yasmine.'

The love of Yasmine's life worked as a geologist at the Mount Isa mines in Queensland and was sometimes away from home for weeks at a time. She and Matt often found themselves unattached at work functions and had forged a friendship. If either had a problem, they used each other as a sounding board.

Didn't mean he wanted to discuss his current problem, but he had a gut feeling he was about to be interrogated as she rounded her desk and accompanied him towards his corner office with its spectacular one-hundred-and-eighty-degree city views.

'Well, aren't you the man?' she said with a smirk, the moment they entered.

He closed his door. Firmly. 'Last time I looked, yes. You have something you want to say, Yaz?'

'You and that little slip of a girl against the wall on Saturday night,' she said cheerfully. 'Then dashing after her that way. Hmm.'

'I wasn't *dashing*.' He felt a prickle between his shoulder-blades and rolled his shoulder. He didn't pursue women. Didn't have to. 'I was making sure she got away safely.' *Hell*. He set his laptop on his desk with a *thunk*, discarded his jacket and laid it carefully across the back of his leather chair. Was it him or was the thermostat set too high in here? 'No law against that, is there?'

She slid her elegant backside onto the corner of his desk. 'No. But…you? You're usually so—' she waved an airy hand '—totally cool and sophisticated and together with women.'

When he didn't reply—because right now he really couldn't think of a comeback—she cocked her head. 'So, what's her name?'

'Ellie.' He switched on his laptop, drumming his fingers on the desk while it booted up. 'Fancy a coffee? It must be break time.'

'Just had one, thanks. Are you seeing her again?'

He shot her a dark look. 'As fate would have it, turns out she works for Belle, so the answer's yes, I'm going to be seeing her again.'

'Fate.' She arched a smooth dark brow at his choice of words, eyes twinkling. 'Serious stuff.'

He shrugged it off. 'Not at all. Just one of life's quirky coincidences.'

'Of all the nightclubs in all of Melbourne...' she purred, leaning closer. 'Yep. Has to be fate.'

'For heaven's sakes, Yaz, give it a rest.'

As always, undeterred by his scowl, Yasmine swung one long leg while she twirled her fingers through a container of paperclips. 'Are you bringing her to the staff do?'

'Staff do?'

'Have you forgotten? You approved the idea. Twenty-first of June—next Monday night for those who forget to look at the calendar. Formal or fancy dress or Celtic, yet to be decided. A money raiser. Charity to be determined by the boss.' She tapped his chest. 'That would be you.'

He grunted. Someone had come up with the idea in February for a winter solstice celebration as a morale booster, he remembered, but he'd been working in Sydney for most of this year and it had slipped his mind.

'So are you going to bring her?' she asked again.

'No.'

'Why not?'

Because...? He preferred the idea of something more inti-mate for their first date, not a roomful of colleagues garnering Ellie's attention. When he and Ellie got together—and they would—he didn't want an audience. 'We're not involved.'

'Yeah, I noticed,' Yasmine said dryly. 'Bring her anyway. Make Belle happy.'

It *would* be a way to keep his word to Belle that he was looking out for Ellie. 'We'll see,' he muttered, more to shut Yasmine up than any promise on his part. But for now... He clicked open a folder on his computer. 'Moving on to more

important matters,' he said, ignoring Yasmine's grin. 'Bring
me up to speed on the Dalton project.'

'Six beers, two tequilas, one rum and Coke,' Ellie recited to
herself, sliding the requested drinks order onto her tray. She
started towards the table of rowdy guys, wishing her black
skirt was a few centimetres longer.

The atmosphere inside the club oozed sweat, cheap
aftershave and testosterone. A lone pole-dancer was doing
her thing to bad music over a poor sound system. According
to Ellie's fellow waitress, Tuesday night wasn't usually busy,
but an entire football team had turned up after training and
were jostling for viewing space.

Her throat felt scratchy with the constant strain of having
to raise her voice over the noise. They were one staff member
short. Sasha, who'd arranged the shift for Ellie and was supposed to be here to help her through the first night, hadn't
turned up. Ellie suppressed her annoyance. Perhaps Sasha
was sick, but she should have phoned.

Well, she was doing just fine tonight without her help,
thank you very much. Only a few more hours with Sleazy
in the cheap business suit mentally undressing her from his
corner table and she was out of here.

She offloaded the beers, carried the rum and Coke to
Sleazy's table.

'How about a nightcap when you finish up here?' he asked
her breasts as she set the glass down.

'No, thanks.' Booze had made him more obnoxious than
he'd been an hour earlier.

'Come on, babe. We'd make a good team, you and me.'

'I don't think so.' She turned to leave but he grasped her
wrist. She wrenched her arm away, toppling his drink. Liquid
splashed the table, sloshing over the edge and onto his shiny
polyester trousers.

'Everything okay, here, Ellie?' A familiar deep voice behind her.

She darted a look over her shoulder, glimpsed Matt and groaned inwardly. With relief, with embarrassment. 'How long have you been here?' And how come she hadn't seen him arrive?

'Long enough.' Then to Sleazy, he leaned low and murmured, 'I suggest you leave while you still can.'

Sleazy glared at Ellie a moment as if deciding to make something of it, then rose. 'You'll pay for this,' he muttered, swiping at the damp patch on his leg. He didn't give eye contact to Matt, she noted, but he sent Ellie a final glare, then pushed his way towards the bar.

'You okay?' She felt Matt's hand at her back but shrugged it off before she did something stupid—like arch against it and purr. 'I'm fine. Please let me get on with my job.'

He stepped back. 'Fine. Get on with it.'

His clipped reply reminded her that she'd been prickly and ungrateful—a survival mechanism, but rude nonetheless—so she followed up with, 'Would you like a drink? On the house.'

He nodded. 'Mineral water. Thanks.'

She watched him return to an empty table on the far side of the room, away from the tables she was serving, and flick open a folder he'd left there. His dark eyes met hers again, sending ripples of awareness down her spine.

Smoothing her skirt, she headed to the bar to place his order and paid for it herself. She couldn't remember the last time someone had bothered to come to her rescue. Even if she hadn't needed it. She reminded herself she didn't need anyone, particularly Matt McGregor, stamping all over her independence.

So when she came by with his drink a few moments later,

she couldn't help herself. 'There are much better strip clubs in town, as I'm sure you—'

'Yes. I know.' He studied her a moment, an almost-grin lurking around his mouth. Then picked up his glass, raised it to her, took a long slow swallow. 'But the evening's young yet.'

Something hot quivered low in her belly, prompting her to say, 'Unless the stripper's a personal friend of yours?' She saw his eyes narrow and leaned towards him a fraction. 'You're checking up on me,' she accused. 'Did you think I was lying to you this morning?'

'Would you lie to me, Ellie?' His gaze slid to her lips. 'About how you feel, for instance?'

Her pulse jumped up a notch and she took a swift step back. Away from the incredible aura he seemed to exude. 'Why would I?'

'Only you can answer that.' Still watching her, he took another swallow from his glass.

'Listen, I don't need a minder—'

'Belle's idea.'

She huffed an impatient breath. 'I'm sure she didn't mean for you to intrude on my private life.'

'I have a moral obligation since I don't consider this a safe working environment. And hasn't that been proven justified?'

She looked away, only to catch the disapproving eye of the bar manager. So it seemed it was okay to be sexually harassed and threatened but chatting with the customers was frowned upon. 'I need to get back to work.'

He set his glass down, flicked an eye over his folder, then drew out his phone. 'And I need to make a call.'

She knew Matt was there, was conscious of his eyes following her for the next couple of hours, even though whenever she glanced his way he had his nose buried in his folder or was speaking into his mobile phone. At one point he was smiling while he talked and she just knew he wasn't talking business—unless it was funny business. And that, she told herself, was none of *her* business.

It was sometime after midnight when the manager paid her at the end of her shift and told her that her services were not required. He told her there'd been a complaint, that she'd come on to a customer, then deliberately spilled his drink when he'd knocked her invitation back. So the manager had docked her the cost of the drink for the damage that the *customer* had caused.

Resentment spiked through her bloodstream. 'That's not how it was and you know it.' Giving him the best evil eye she could manage, she stuffed what was left of her night's pay into her bag, buttoned her coat with quick jerky movements. 'You can take your lousy job and stick it in a very dark place,' she snapped out on her way to the nearest exit.

Ellie was accustomed to people expecting her to be an easy walkover. Usually she fought back. She could have argued her case; she was the injured party here. Tonight, as she manoeuvred her way through testosterone city, all she wanted to do was get out of this pit and lay her throbbing head on a pillow and sleep for a week. Was she coming down with a bug?

She shook it away. Not going to happen. She had to rise and shine early tomorrow. At this point she really, really needed Belle's part-time job. And *now* it came with an additional problem... Speaking of which, did she say goodbye to Matt or what? Would he think she was angling for a lift home? Or more? She glanced to where he'd been sitting moments earlier but he'd left. Without a word.

Good, she told herself as she veered back towards the exit. One less problem. Tomorrow morning was way soon enough to be interacting with him. She wasn't in the mood to deal with complications. And despite his views about their *non-*

relationship, Matt McGregor was *complication* in flashing lights. Big red warning ones.

Doing his gentlemanly duty as he saw Ellie preparing to leave, he exited the bar and waited for her outside.

She'd told him she wanted to be left alone, but safety concerns aside, knowing where she'd be this evening had been too much of a temptation for Matt to ignore. He'd wanted to see her again, simple as that. He stepped towards her the moment she appeared. 'I'll walk you to your car.'

Her head swivelled towards him and her eyes widened. 'Why are you still here?'

The damp air teased her hair so that it curled in wisps around her face. She must have washed it again because it was lighter—honey blonde with only a streak or two of pink—but the austere light from the street lamp turned it silver-white, making her appear smaller, more fragile.

'You think I'd leave you here at this time of night without ensuring your safe journey home?' Wherever that might be.

She pulled her coat tighter, straightened her spine, hitched her bag higher. 'I can take care of myself.'

'Yeah, right. Alone, past midnight, in this seedy area. Where's your car?'

'I don't own a car. And I happen to live in this seedy area.' He didn't miss the light of contempt in her eyes.

Along with her list of criticisms, did she think him prejudiced? He couldn't decide whether it amused or annoyed him. 'How are you getting home?'

'Public transport.'

'My car's across the road. I'll drop you off.'

'It's—'

'Non-negotiable.' He placed a silencing finger against her lips.

Heat, as her sharp exhalation of breath streamed over his

fingertip. Friction, as his finger drifted lightly over her lips. Desire, sharp and swift, as her lips parted the tiniest bit. In surprise? Or something else? He couldn't be sure, and for a pulse beat or two he thought she might yield and open further. But she remained completely still.

'Non-negotiable, Ellie.' He pressed his thumb to her lower lip, watching her eyes darken to an intense charcoal in the dimness. 'So get used to the idea quickly.'

CHAPTER FOUR

ELLIE didn't move, didn't pull away, even as a throng of raucous patrons spilled from the bar and ambled past, their voices raised in some tuneless song. The night breeze, pungent with the sting of exhaust fumes, wrapped around them. In the distance an alarm wailed. He wanted to press his momentary advantage, replace his thumb with his mouth and relive that first kiss.

He could almost smell the desire on her skin, but he didn't push it. She stepped back, eyes flicking away, as if giving him eye contact might betray her. She scanned the row of parked cars. 'Let me guess—yours is the champagne-tinted convertible.'

'Sorry to disappoint—it's the little bent and black ninety-six Ford.' He couldn't resist adding, 'My Ferrari's in Sydney.'

Her laugh was spontaneous and unexpected and she seemed as surprised as he. 'I *knew* it,' she said with a half-smile. 'Red?'

'Is there any other colour?' With a light hand at her back, he steered her across the road.

Ellie practically fell onto the seat, willing her pulse to settle down while Matt rounded the car. Good Lord, just that single thumb print on her lower lip had turned her inside out. If he hadn't stopped—oh, she did not want to think about it. He made her weak. Made her want…what she couldn't have.

By the time he'd climbed into his seat she'd managed to halfway calm herself. She directed him to a street about a kilometre away. She spent a moment studying the car's interior rather than the width of Matt's more than capable hands on the steering wheel, focusing on the engine's rough-throated purr rather than the scent of clean masculine skin.

But as they neared her apartment her breathing changed for very different reasons. And with every passing moment the band beneath her breastbone tightened.

She'd always sensed Heath's low opinion of her previous apartment even though he'd never voiced it. As if her living conditions reflected her worth as a human being. She might have been in love with him but her self-confidence and sense of self-worth had taken a battering and never fully recovered. Compared to this dump it had been a palace.

Would Matt the squillionaire businessman judge her the same way? And why did it suddenly seem to matter if he did? 'You can drop me off here,' she said, ready to jump out and flee the moment they stopped.

The building she lived in was crammed between the abandoned car park of a graffiti-covered warehouse and a row of currently untenanted shops.

Matt slowed to a stop. 'This your place?'

His tone didn't change but her stomach clenched tighter. 'Yes.' She knew what he was thinking. She just knew it. She would *not* let it bring her down.

She reached for the doorhandle. Before she could thank him and escape, he was out of the car and rounding the bonnet.

'No need to see me inside—I live upstairs,' she said, climbing out. Somewhere nearby a cat yowled and the din of metal rolling down the street broke the night's stillness.

'How long have you lived here?'

'A couple of months.' She remembered him quipping about his Ferrari. 'Would it help if I said I used to live in Toorak?'

she said, forcing humour into her voice as she mentioned one of Melbourne's most affluent suburbs.

He didn't return her smile. 'Only if it helps *you*.'

It didn't and her smile faded. Those days were gone. Once upon a time, before the people she loved had been erased from her life for ever, her world had been very different.

But his voice helped. Smooth and steady and even, like a still lake, soothing the rough edges around her heart. Until she looked up into his eyes and saw the storm, all dark and brooding and beautiful. Reminding her that she didn't want to get involved. With anyone, ever again.

'Thanks for the lift.' She paused before adding, 'And thanks for your assistance at the bar tonight.'

'No worries.' He didn't seem in a hurry to leave.

She hesitated. 'I'll see you tomorrow, then.'

He nodded. 'You're coming. Good.'

'I didn't get the bar job, so yes.' She shrugged, trying for philosophical, failing miserably.

'Because it wasn't the right job for you.' There was something in his eyes. Not sympathy—she didn't want sympathy, nor did she need it. Understanding?

She stood, rooted to the spot, watching him while he jingled his car keys. What the hell would he understand about the tough non-corporate world of low finance?

'Goodnight, Ellie.' He touched his lips to hers. A token kiss, almost impersonal. No sexual undertones. Nothing she could call him on.

And nothing to get herself in a lather about.

Because now he'd watched her lose a job on the first night and seen where she lived, what other kind of kiss could it be?

She stepped away before she kissed him back and made it into something it wasn't. 'Goodnight.'

She turned abruptly and made it through the entry door and

halfway along the common hallway before the door behind her opened again. She looked over her shoulder. Matt's silhouette filled the space and a thrill of excitement shivered down her spine before she could stop it. 'Is something wrong?'

'Damn right something's wrong.' He stepped inside and walked towards her, his shoes echoing on the worn concrete floor, his features growing clearer as he neared. 'I should be ashamed of myself. Kissing you that way.'

Huh? Her mouth fell open in astonishment and she remained where she was, sure her heartbeat would wake the entire building. 'It's okay.' The words trembled out. 'I didn't—'

'Since when do you let a guy kiss you like that and get away with it?' He gripped her shoulders. Walked her back until her shoulders touched the wall, eyes glittering in the dim stairwell's light. His face was close, his hands possessive, stroking down her upper arms.

With what little strength she had left, she hugged her handbag in front of her like a shield. 'Depends… On who's doing the kissing.' Oh, good Lord, had she said that aloud, and in that thin reedy voice that seemed to be coming from someone else?

His sensuous lips curved and he moved nearer. His jeans brushed against her bare legs. Hard thighs rubbed hers…and heat speared into her lower belly. Her arms slid uselessly to her sides, leaving her bag dangling from one shoulder.

'I am,' he murmured before his mouth descended on hers.

She could no more hold back her response than stop the sun from rising. Her lips fell open beneath his and her whole body shuddered against him. Without any idea of how they got there, her hands slid to his waist and grasped fistfuls of his shirt beneath his jacket.

His taste was as she remembered, only more. Richer, fuller, more intoxicating—

'Excuse me, Ellie… Perhaps you could take your displays of…affection upstairs?'

Ellie jerked back, her head bouncing off the wall. 'Um, hi. Mrs Green.' From apartment two. And looking less than impressed that they were all but standing in front of her door. Ducking under Matt's arm, Ellie spun away into the passage, fumbling with her slippery hold on her bag at the same time. 'Um. Sorry.'

Matt and Ellie regarded each other without speaking until her downstairs neighbour's door closed and they were alone again.

It gave Ellie time to gather her jumbled thoughts. She considered it a minor miracle that she was able to say, 'It's late and I'm tired,' in a reasonably steady no-nonsense voice. And she meant it. Every muscle felt sapped of energy and she had no idea whether it was Matt's fault or the bug she seemed to be coming down with.

Matt, who'd propped himself against the wall, watched her with a hint of the devil in his eyes. 'Mrs Green's suggestion sounds good to me.'

'Not to me.' Straightening, she pulled out her keys. 'I've worked two jobs today. Goodnight, Matt.' She caught a glimpse of that sexy grin before she forced herself to turn away and head for the stairs.

It was way, way harder than she wanted it to be.

Ellie was woken by a dull throbbing headache when her alarm trilled at 7:00 a.m. And when she swallowed, it was like forcing a razor blade down her throat. To her surprise, she realised she'd slept the entire night, probably because she'd been so exhausted.

So how come she felt as if she hadn't slept a wink?

With a groan, she dragged herself out of bed and peered through her dust-spattered window at the heavy-bellied clouds just visible in the dawn sky. A dark rain shower swept across the distant suburbs, wind whistled with malice around the ill-fitting pane.

A perfect day to burrow back under her quilt and nurse her sore throat. But she didn't have that luxury, so she grabbed a couple of painkillers at the kitchen sink before stumbling to the bathroom.

She stepped beneath the ancient showerhead, shivering as she soaped up quickly under the meagre lukewarm stream. She'd just bet Matt McGregor was still tucked up nice and warm in *his* bed.

And after that kiss last night...well, she might have been sharing it with him. His hot, hard body pressing her into the mattress, springy masculine hair rasping against her nipples. That deep voice, gravelly with sleep and sinful suggestions while his fingers played out those sinful suggestions over her—

'Get those X-rated thoughts of your *employer's nephew* right out of your head,' she ordered herself, whipping the shower curtain aside, creating a shivery draught. Grabbing her towel, she rubbed briskly to get the blood flowing beneath her skin. 'Concentrate on important matters. Like an income.'

Belle paid her generously, but she needed to supplement it with another part-time job and somehow fit both jobs in around the volunteer after-school shifts she worked at the children's centre around the corner.

She loved kids but she'd never fall in love again, could never risk a failed marriage. Which meant no children, ever. But her maternal instincts were very much alive, and working with underprivileged children was her way of satisfying that natural urge.

Grabbing a muesli bar, she swung her gear onto her shoulder and headed out into the wintry day. The tram was crowded and stuffy with early-morning commuters, and Ellie was glad of the fresh air when she disembarked just after eight and walked the last few minutes to Belle's place.

Remembering yesterday, she knocked on the back door to let Matt know she'd arrived. She could always hope he'd already gone to work. On the other hand she could hope she'd gotten him out of bed. To see him dishevelled and disgruntled at her early arrival. Bleary-eyed, unshaven…

'Good morning, Ellie.'

She turned at his voice. He was none of those things.

Fully dressed in dark jeans and a soft-looking cream jumper that probably cost more than her entire wardrobe, he ambled from the garage, morning newspaper and a carton of milk in hand. He'd obviously showered and shaved already; the fresh smell of sandalwood soap carried on the breeze. And his eyes were bright, alert and focused. On her.

Memories of last night's kiss hung in the air between them. But this was a working day, a working environment, and she intended keeping it that way.

'Good morning.' She cleared her throat, wincing at the raw pain as she did so and trotted down the back steps with an officious, 'I'll be getting on with it, then.'

'Want a coffee before you start?'

'No, thanks. I want to make some headway before it starts to rain.'

'What are your plans today?'

'I have to finish digging over the plot.' Which she should have finished yesterday, but with Matt calling the meeting and all, it had put her behind. She kept moving, walking backwards as she spoke. 'Then it's the fertiliser and seedlings— Belle left everything in the greenhouse. Are you going to the office?'

'I don't plan on it,' he said, dashing her hopes for a day

without the prospect of further interruptions. 'I've a costing to finish and a computer link-up with the Sydney crew.'

She nodded. 'I'll come by the door when I'm done.'

When she stopped for lunch, she ate her sandwich and drank her thermos of coffee alone. Despite what she'd told Matt about being self-sufficient, Belle always invited Ellie inside to share her break.

On the last day Ellie had seen her, Belle had offered her a key to the main house, allowing her access to the bathroom and hot water. But she'd felt awkward about the whole idea and refused it. If anything happened in Belle's absence Ellie didn't want to be held responsible; it was bad enough that she'd given her the code to the gate.

She'd not glimpsed Matt since she'd started work this morning. Seemed he was in accord with her—business hours were just that. She didn't know whether she was relieved or disappointed.

Her mobile rang as she was packing away her lunch box. She glanced at caller ID and answered straightaway. 'Sasha. I tried calling you last night. Where did you get to?'

'I called in sick. I just opened your message.'

Her friend sounded distant and Ellie felt that all-too-familiar clutch in her belly. 'Are you okay now?'

'Never better.'

'So are you up to checking out that Healesville job with me sometime soon? We need to let them know—'

'Ah, about that...' A pause, then Sasha went into excitement mode with, 'I met this great guy at a club last night. Anyway...' she went on when Ellie didn't reply, 'I've got the chance to work onboard a cruise ship leaving Sydney in a week's time.'

Disappointment ripped through Ellie. 'I thought you said you were sick last night?'

'Everyone chucks a sickie now and then, right?'

No. Not when it mattered they didn't. 'I was counting on you to show me the ropes at the bar last night.'

'Oh. Sorry. Did you get the job, by the way?'

'Let's just say I'm not cut out for that sort of waitressing. Which is why this Healesville job is important to me.' She closed her eyes, surrendered to the inevitable. 'Sasha, obviously your heart's not in this, so take the cruise job and forget Healesville.' *Forget everything.*

The bed-and-breakfast place out of Melbourne was offering a four-week stint to landscape their garden, and Ellie had persuaded Sasha to come along. Ellie had explained that she didn't want to let Belle down while she was away and had promised to get back to them by the end of next week. She intended winning the job, with or without Sasha.

'Hey, you there, Ellie?'

'I'm here.'

'So…I'll call you when I get back and maybe we can—'

'There's no point, Sasha, it's just not practical. Good luck with everything. Goodbye.' *And have a nice life.* She stabbed the disconnect button.

She'd thought they were friends. But true friends didn't let each other down. When was she going to learn? Ellie had some kind of in-built radar that sent people running in the opposite direction.

Remember that when you think about Matt McGregor.

As befitting her mood, ten minutes later it started to spit—a cold, ugly, misty spit. Ellie pulled on her thin plastic poncho and continued digging. She would *not* quit on account of rain. Unlike Sasha, she'd prove herself reliable and responsible and accountable if it killed her.

Matt pulled himself mentally and physically out of his work. He glanced at his watch, surprised to find he'd worked through the lunch break he'd set himself. He'd intended talking Ellie into sharing a coffee. Stretching fingers cramped from work-ing the keyboard, he wrapped them around his neck and glanced at the window. Rain spattered the glass.

He walked to the kitchen window and saw her. Mud splattered her overalls up to her knees. She was measuring and pouring pellets into her hand, sprinkling them over the earth, then moving on to repeat the procedure. The misty rain speckled the flimsy plastic she'd pulled on but the cap had blown off, leaving dark honey locks damp and curling over her head.

His gaze narrowed. Yesterday he'd raised the question of her responsibility. After all, it was she who'd labelled herself irresponsible. Was she now trying to prove a point? Responsible was all well and good, but there wasn't much point to it if the woman came down with pneumonia.

He stalked to the back door, grabbing an umbrella from the coat stand on the way. Rain spattered his soft leather shoes. It wasn't heavy but constant, and obviously had been for some time. But the wind was fierce—it snuck under the umbrella, threatening to turn it inside out.

She was facing away from him and didn't hear his ap-proach. Or was she choosing not to?

'Why the hell are you still out here in this weather?' He reached for her shoulder to swing her around but she squealed and jerked and he lost his footing in the slimy mud her dig-ging had created. The umbrella was forgotten as he fought the inevitable and ignominious slide to the ground, taking her with him.

At the last second he managed to twist them both so that she landed on top of him in a blur of limbs and bad language. While he was still trying to catch his breath, he stared up at the rain-spattered sky, contemplating this example of life's little jokes. Cold muddy moisture seeped through the back of his jumper, a striking contrast to the warm wet body plastered against his chest.

When she didn't move, he raised his head and wheezed, 'You all right?'

'Oh, yeah, never better,' she snapped. Apparently unconcerned that he might be on his last breath, her only movement was to disentangle her legs from his and tug on the strap of her overalls.

He would have laughed at the situation but what air was left in his lungs exploded out of him as her elbow jabbed him in the solar plexus.

'Sorry.' She twisted some more, the sound of plastic crinkling as she continued struggling to free herself. He didn't try to help. Giving up the attempt for the moment, she glared down at him. '*What* were you thinking?'

Rain-spiked lashes blinked at him over those gorgeous lilac-coloured eyes. When he could breathe again, he smelled summer raspberries and her own brand of hot feminine scent. The scent a woman exudes after a healthy bout of exercise. Or sex. He took this unique opportunity to draw it in slowly.

What had she said? Something about thinking… 'I wasn't.' If he'd been *thinking* he'd have engineered this scenario somewhere dry—on Belle's Persian rug in front of a roaring fire, for instance. Minus the wet clothing.

'I was reacting,' he continued, 'to your hare-brained idea of working outdoors in these conditions.'

'It's where most gardening's done.' She rolled a shoulder, the movement shifting her breasts against his stomach. He wasn't sure, but he imagined he could feel two stiff nipples jutting just above his navel.

A spear of heat shot through his body, angling straight to his groin. Doing his damnedest to ignore it, he stared up at the sky again and continued with, 'So is this your attempt to prove you're responsible or stubborn or both?'

Her hips chafed against his as she dragged a trapped hand from between their bodies to push at her crinkled hair. 'What's a little rain, for heaven's sakes?'

His gaze shifted to her face. To her eyes, irises dark with some unnamed emotion she refused to admit to. Her mouth, damp with rain and a tempting whisper from his own. He could kiss her now, drink in the freshness of raindrops and Ellie. 'For one thing, it's wet. And damn cold.'

She stared back at him, shook her head. 'You indoor career types are too soft.'

He didn't feel soft. And if she didn't quit squirming against him like that she was going to find that out for herself.

And bingo: She went completely still, and when he looked, her eyes had widened. He watched the colour intensify, her cheeks turn a shade pinker before she scrambled up on her knees and pushed away. Up. Pieces of her now-shredded plastic poncho flapped like flags in the wind.

'Stubborn, then,' he muttered. He pushed up too, his jumper peeling away from the mud with a slimy sound. An instant chill cloaked his body. 'We'd better get out of these wet clothes.'

Without looking at him she picked up her trowel. 'You go ahead, I need to clean up here first.'

'Leave it, I'll come out later and tidy up.'

'My job, I'll do it.'

'Fine. Catch pneumonia.'

Without looking at him, she stacked everything in the barrow, including the mangled umbrella, with infuriating slowness, then wheeled it to the garden shed. So be it. He could be as ridiculously stubborn about this as she.

He waited until she locked up, put the key in its hidey-hole, then took her sweet time walking back with her pack on her shoulder. Even from metres away he could see she was shivering, that now the blush had faded, her cheeks were pale and there were dark circles beneath her eyes.

He met her halfway across the lawn. He didn't think about whether she'd object, just took her chilled wet hand in his. 'Come on.' He hustled her up the path to the verandah, pulling away the plastic remains of her poncho as they shuffled under shelter and into the laundry. 'A hot shower will warm you up. Or a bath. Whichever you prefer.'

'No. I'll be all right.'

'Ellie.' Concerned now, he shot her a stern look. 'You're wet through. You're going to take that shower if I have to put you under it myself.' He peeled off his sodden jumper, tossed it on the floor.

Her gaze slid like a hot silk glove down his chest. He was about to make a joke of it all, but something warned him she wouldn't see the humour right now. She gulped, then lifted panicked eyes to his. 'I'm all muddy.'

'That you are. I'll find you some of Belle's clothes.'

She shook her head. 'I'm not trailing mud and water all through the house.'

'Take off your shoes.' He stepped out of his, removed his socks.

Ellie did the same, then looked up at him. *Not* looking at that gloriously exposed chest. Oh, why had she thought working in the rain was a good idea? At the time she hadn't given any thought to the mud factor. Nor had she counted on them wallowing in it. Together. 'My shoes aren't the only things covered in mud.'

She regretted those words instantly. She felt the heat in his gaze as it travelled over the rest of her and wondered why her clothes weren't steaming.

'Same here.' If anything, he was in a worse state than her. The entire length of him was iced in shiny brown mud. He unsnapped his sodden jeans.

Ah… 'What are you doing?'

'Someone has to do *something* if we're going to find clean dry clothes,' he said, being entirely too practical.

It took a moment for him to ease his jeans over his hips and step out of them. Involuntarily—that's what she told herself—her eyes followed his fingers down the length of his strongly muscled thighs and over his knees to the hairy calves and long knobbly toes as he shucked the denim off.

And, oh… My goodness. Except for a pair of navy boxers which rode low on his lean hips, he was stark-staring naked. She sucked in a breath.

Imagine him naked.

But the perfection of his golden-toned body was even better than her imagination had been able to conjure up. She could smell his skin. Two steps closer and she'd be able to reach out and touch. Another step and she'd be able to taste.

No. If she let him close again, she was going to fall for him; she just knew it. And it would be a much harder landing than that soft mudslide a few moments ago. Safer to keep her distance. And the only way to keep that distance was to *not* give him any encouragement.

If he'd noticed her indulging in her little fantasy, he didn't show it. He was all matter of fact and purpose, rescuing his clothes from the floor and dumping them in the laundry trough.

Ellie remained where she was. Did he expect her to follow his lead? She could take off her overalls and still be no more exposed than she would in her bikini…but that wasn't going to happen. Not with Matt McGregor watching on.

'Use this,' he said, handing her a sheet which he pulled from a nearby cupboard. 'You can slip out of your things and wrap it around you. When you're ready, meet me in the kitchen.'

Moments later, down to her underwear, and clutching the

sheet around her, Ellie followed Matt through a formal lounge and dining room. If she could just keep her sex-starved eyes off his broad-shouldered, near-naked body along the way... She bit back a sigh at the way the light played over the muscles beneath that healthy olive-toned skin and his hairy masculine thighs before making a conscious effort to avert her gaze.

She'd never been upstairs, but as she followed Matt, it was clear Belle paid the same loving attention to detail throughout the grand old house. She passed a pretty feminine bedroom, then a bedroom with a huge four-poster bed and a mountain of maroon quilt. A pair of shiny black men's shoes were placed neatly on the floor at the foot of the bed. A perfectly pressed snowy shirt hung on a hanger on the wardrobe door.

Matt slept in this room.

Her blood thickened and, without realising, she slowed, hoping for a glimpse of something that told her more about the man beyond the obvious fact that he was tidy. She shook it away, reminding herself she knew all she needed to know. She wasn't here for a tour. She was here to get clean.

'This is the guest room,' Matt said, opening a door further down. 'The en suite's through there.' He gestured to another door on the far side of the room. 'You should find everything you need. Meanwhile I'll rustle up some clothes and leave them on the bed for you. When you're done, can you find your way back to the kitchen?'

'Yes. Thank you.'

'Take your time.'

She didn't reply, just waited until he left before relaxing enough to take it all in. Beautiful in shades of green and white and gold. Big double bed, snow-white quilt. Elegant pictures of a bygone era on the walls. A view over the rose garden, dark spikes now, in the dead of winter.

In the bathroom, light spilled through a skylight, bathing a froth of fernery in one corner. She flicked a switch and an instant flood of heat rolled over her shoulders. Absolute decadence.

There was a double-headed shower and a bath big enough for three. The bath won. When it was full she sank in and let frangipani-scented bubbles soak away the grime.

Not so easy to soak away thoughts of Matt and the way their bodies had clashed out there in the muddy garden plot. It put another spin on getting down and dirty.

He'd been turned on.

At the memory of that hard, hot masculine wedge beneath her a bolt of heat shot to her core. Had he been turned on before or after she'd wiggled? And she'd reacted to that subtle prod like a frightened virgin.

Which was best all-round, she decided, diverting her concentration to scrubbing her skin until it tingled. It would give him yet another reason to think she wasn't interested in him and leave her alone.

Admit it, Ellie. You want him. You want him bad.

As her sex slave, she told herself. That was all. That was *all*?

Yes, she decided, swirling the bubbles through her fingers, *turn the social tables on him.* So...if he was in here with her... She flopped back against the bath's edge. She'd command him to start with her back. Keeping the best bits for last. Keeping the delicious anticipation to the max.

She have him kneel behind her, so close that she'd hear his heart beating, feel his breath against her hair. He'd lave beneath her ear, move on to her neck, her collarbone. Then he'd soap up those long, tanned fingers and drag them over her shoulders, down her breasts, stopping to massage her nipples, draw them out. Slowly...

She sneezed, an unwelcome explosion, dragging her out of the moment and back to reality.

And that reality appeared to be that she was, indeed,

coming down with a bug. She could not afford to get sick. She needed as much work as she could get. Which reminded her she was in her employer's bathroom, using Belle's lotions and potions and fantasising about her nephew. For goodness' sake.

She yanked out the plug and snatched one of the thick jade towels off the rack. Damn Matt. For making her want things she had no business wanting. Her employer's nephew. A man way out of her league.

Impossible.

CHAPTER FIVE

MATT knocked at the partially open bedroom door. When there was no answer, he entered carefully. He'd found one of Belle's jumpers, a pair of soft jersey sweatpants and thick socks. As for underwear… She'd have to go commando for now.

And wouldn't that be something to think about over steak and salad? He should have put the items on the bed and left, but the sweet floral scent seeping from beneath the door was too tempting to resist.

It had been a long time since his own bathroom had smelled like this. Feminine. Alluring. Inviting…

When he and Angela had shared an apartment. His jaw clenched. Those times were over. These days when he took a lover, it was his way or the highway. They used her place. He rarely slept the night. Sleeping implied a degree of intimacy he simply didn't have. Didn't want. Didn't need.

He breathed the scent in again, deeply. What did he know of the girl on the other side of that door? By her own admission, she was a drifter. How long before she up and left? Where did she go and what did she do, and who did she do it with while she was there?

Still… Until then, he didn't see a problem with them sharing something a little more personal when the gardening tools were packed away for the evening. And he could keep his word to Belle at the same time.

Unfortunately it couldn't be tonight. He'd organised a meeting with the construction manager on one of his latest Melbournian projects but Cole had been tied up elsewhere until this evening. They'd arranged to meet over a beer later.

He didn't intend to start something with Ellie tonight and not be able to finish it. When he got her naked, he wanted everything right. He wanted to take it slow, enjoy—

The sound of the bathroom door opening warned him to leave but it was already too late. Ellie wafted out on a cloud of scented steam and he waged a quick tug of war within himself. Her stifled yelp and the way she stood clutching her towel and damp underwear almost had a grin tugging at his mouth.

Until he got a better look at what she held in her hand. Fire-engine-red G-string, matching satin and lace bra. Surprise. Who'd have thought that beneath those ugly overalls…?

Remember Saturday night?

This was that same woman, and his pulse quickened, his mood sobering to something darker as the primitive side of him stirred to life. Her skin glowed a delicate peach. He imagined it was as soft and luscious as it looked. It took all his will not to stride right over there and sample it. Her legs, bared to her upper thigh, were perfection and she reminded him of a long-stemmed rose on a foggy day.

He couldn't seem to look away. Couldn't move. Felt as if his body had turned to stone. Inside his skin was another matter. His mouth was dry and his blood was surging south. Somehow he remembered why he was there, cleared his throat and lifted the bundle of clothes in his hands. 'I'll just put these on the bed.… I've put the rest of your clothes in the washing machine. Would you like me to add those?' He gestured to her bundle.

'No.'

Her fingers tightened into a fist around it and he got that she was thinking of his hands on her G-string.

He almost groaned aloud. *Way* bad timing. A fleeting thought that he could ring Cole and postpone darted through his mind, but their meeting was important and he was a professional first and foremost. Business took priority.

'Okay.' He swallowed, then continued with, 'If the trousers are too long you can roll the legs up or whatever....' He thought it wiser not to mention underwear again.

'Thanks.' She didn't move. 'Was there something else?'

'I'm fixing us a bite to eat when you're ready. How do you like your steak?'

'Steak?'

'You're not vegetarian, are you?'

'No, rare, and why are we having this conversation right here, *right now*?'

'Rare. Okay.' He made himself step back. 'I'll leave you to it, then.'

The instant he'd gone, Ellie rushed to the door and locked it before the man decided to come back to ask her wine preferences. He was fixing steak? For her? For *them*?

Dropping the towel, she hauled on the clothes he'd provided her with. In front of the mirror, she ran a comb through her unruly hair, then, with no hair straighteners in sight, gave it up as a lost cause. And what did it matter? She didn't care what Matt McGregor thought. Nor was she going to be impressed—or swayed—by his cooking prowess. She stuffed her damp undies in her backpack and started down the hallway, following the aroma of frying onions.

When she entered the kitchen Matt already had the steaks on the grill and was chopping tomatoes into a salad bowl. His freshly shampooed hair gleamed under the light and he wore another of those soft-looking jumpers.

She looked around for something to do. 'You want me to finish that?'

'All under control.' He inclined his head towards a jug of juice topped with mint leaves and ice. 'Help yourself.'

'Thank you.' She noted he already had one at his elbow and poured herself a glass. She felt dumb standing around without a task so she hefted herself onto a breakfast stool. 'Do you cook often?'

'Not as often as I like. Too busy. This week's going to give me a good opportunity. You?'

'Hate it.' She sipped the juice. Freshly juiced orange, pine-apple and passionfruit. 'This is nice.'

'Juicing it at home's a vast improvement over supermarket brands. So…Ellie.' Multi-tasking Matt gave the onions a stir, flipped the steaks, reached for the cucumber. 'You mentioned you lived around here as a child. Do your parents still live in Melbourne?'

'No.' She didn't want to talk about her parents. It reminded her of how alone she was. But in the ensuing silence she knew courtesy demanded an elaboration of sorts. 'Mum and my grandparents died in a car accident more than eighteen years ago.'

His knife paused midslice, a measured compassion in his dark eyes. 'I'm sorry, Ellie. That must've been tough. How old were you?'

'Six.' A misty image of her mother singing a lullaby stole through her mind and her heart twisted. Even after all this time, the pain would shoot back at the most unexpected times.

'After, it was just my father and me for a couple of years travelling country Victoria and South Australia while he took the odd job….' *Then played the odd game of chance and lost what he'd earned.* She didn't tell him her father had only come back into her life when Mum had died.

Before Matt could ask, she said, 'In the end I held him back.'

He looked up sharply. 'What do you mean, you "held him back"? He was your father.'

'He couldn't look for work and care for me.' But deep down that nine-year-old inside her still cried. *He could have if he'd wanted to.*

Matt turned to slide the steaks onto two plates, muttering something she was better off not hearing. Because then she'd want to defend her father and tell Matt she'd forgive him in a moment if he ever came back. *She was that weak.*

She often wondered if that's why she felt compelled to move around the country. Was she hoping to find him? Or was she running from him? Running from any involvement that might tear open those childhood wounds that had never quite healed.

She turned the focus to him, or rather, away from her. 'What about your parents?'

His lips tightened as he set the sizzling plates on the breakfast bar. 'It's just me and Belle.'

Old pain. She heard it in his voice. Tight and angry. Saw it in his avoidance of eye contact. Recognised it because she lived with it herself, every day.

He pushed the salad bowl her way. 'Help yourself.'

'Thanks. Avocadoes too—my favourite,' she said to lighten the atmosphere as she spooned salad onto her plate.

So he didn't want to talk about it. She understood that. Men didn't delve into personal and emotional issues. Matt's mother's absence in his life—for whatever reason that he wasn't inclined to share with her—had left scars. As it would, of course. But she had a feeling it went much deeper than grief. There was a bitterness and anger there too.

They ate in silence for a few moments, listening to the

sound of the rain lashing the window. The stormy weather had intensified over the past hour.

'Do you ever—' The jingle of Matt's mobile phone in the adjoining room cut Ellie off.

'Excuse me.'

Matt rose, leaving her alone in the kitchen with a jumble of thoughts running through her head. The family he didn't want to discuss and the walls he'd erected.

He'd made no attempt to disguise his attraction to her, but obviously that was as far as it went. His interest was purely physical. Unfortunately it was becoming more and more obvious that, for her, it went beyond that. His sheer magnetism drew her, sparking an undercurrent of excitement which flowed constantly just beneath the surface of her skin, so strong she wondered that she didn't glow in the dark, and leaving her in a perpetual state of anticipation. She'd never known anything this intense.

But despite his unwillingness to open up, he also had a nurturing, caring side no other male had ever shown her. In fact, he could be downright chivalrous, and that was so… attractive. Seductive. Alluring as it was alarming.

Which meant she needed to be on her guard at all times.

His voice carried through the open doorway. She heard the name of a five-star hotel mentioned. And then the lobby at 8:00 p.m. He'd be a little later than they'd arranged. Unavoidably detained… Looking forward to catching up…

Was his tone an indication that he was talking to a woman or did he speak to everyone in that deep velvet voice? She didn't know him well enough to tell…was this just Ellie being slightly paranoid Ellie?

'Matthew's always been a bit of a playboy….'

Something hard and heavy lobbed dead centre in her chest. She jabbed the point of her knife into her half-eaten steak, hacked off a piece, jammed it in her mouth. Why the hell did it matter who he met? She chewed vigorously. Or what he did with whomever it was tonight? At 8:00 p.m. In one of the best hotels in the city.

She tried to swallow but the food lodged behind the knot which had formed in her throat over the past couple of minutes.

'Meat not to your liking?' Matt took his seat once more and resumed eating.

'It's…very nice,' she managed and swallowed carefully. 'Just a bit of a sore throat.' She reached for her juice to wash it down. 'I need an early night. In fact…' She made a show of glancing at her watch, didn't note the time. 'I'll get going. There's a tram due in ten minutes. I'll collect my other clothes later.'

'I'll drop you home.'

'Not necessary, I've an umbrella in my bag.' *And you have a date.*

'I insist. I have to go out in any case—I'll drop you off on the way. Just give me a moment.'

She accepted because she really didn't feel one hundred percent and it was easier than arguing. But she almost changed her mind when he reappeared in dark trousers and a smart charcoal jacket that looked as if it had been tailored exclusively for him. A few wisps of masculine hair were visible at the open neck of his shirt.

He'd splashed on that cologne she'd smelled the other night. Something free and fresh and foresty that reminded her of secret midnight trysts.

She thought about that—and him—when she climbed into her narrow bed after he'd dropped her outside her apartment building a short time later. And reminded herself that permanent playboys were not for her.

* * *

Matt rolled over, peered at the digital readout on his clock and swore. Seven-thirty.

He dragged a hand over his face. He felt as if he hadn't caught more than ten minutes' shut-eye at any one time. Erotic dreams had plagued him from the moment his head had hit the pillow. The kind of dreams he'd not experienced since puberty.

Ellie was entirely to blame.

Pushing the quilt down to cool his overheated body, he stared at the ceiling's blank canvas, hoping to rid himself of the images still dancing behind his eyes.

No such luck. It didn't make a scrap of difference that he'd chatted up a tall well-constructed New York advertising executive after his meeting with Cole. Lysandra. Lissendra? He'd bought her a cocktail and they'd discussed… Global warming. A couple of cocktails on, she'd had a few interesting suggestions to help cure his insomnia. And he'd come close to letting her try.

Until a vision of Ellie Rose wearing nothing but that towel had sauntered into his mind like a siren from days gone by… He sat up in bed, scratched his morning stubble. Damn it.

Since when had he turned down a woman like Lissandra whose requirements ticked all the right boxes? Why would he pass up an opportunity like that for a girl who didn't want to get involved, despite her eyes and the way she kissed telling him otherwise? A girl nothing like the women he dated.

And that girl would be turning up at any moment, if she wasn't here already. Easing off the bed, he padded down the passage and into a spare bedroom for a view of the backyard. Low on the horizon, the early morning's thin lemon sunlight was sliding obliquely between the clouds, glistening wetly on the lawn. He scanned the boggy patch where Ellie had been working yesterday. The garden shed. The back porch.

No sign of her.

She'd be here, he told himself; she wanted the job. Still, he felt oddly disappointed she hadn't arrived yet. He wanted to see that glimpse of sunshine turn her hair to old gold and watch the jaunty, carefree way she had of moving.

He folded his arms across his chest as chilly air prickled his skin. Yeah, right. Watching her while he stood here naked. Scowling, he scrubbed a hand over his jaw. *Lucky for you, you're not here yet, Ellie Rose.*

Meanwhile he needed a cold shower and he needed it fast.

While he shivered and soaped up under the spray, he made a decision. This thing between them needed serious attention. Tonight. Get it out of their systems—two rational, consenting adults—then they could move on.

He turned off the taps, reached for his towel. Satisfied with his plan, he lathered on shaving cream and reached for his razor.

He checked his emails over fruit and toast. Coffee in hand, he made a follow-up call to last night's meeting with Cole. Then he phoned the office to inform Joanie he'd be in before ten and took the next little while to look over a new project.

When Ellie still hadn't turned up by nine o'clock he grew annoyed. He paced to the window. The devil of it was, he had no good reason to be so ticked off. Ellie kept her own timetable and Belle hadn't expected him to wait around. But he was here now, and in Belle's absence he felt he was entitled to know Ellie's plans for today. Keep an eye on things. Keep his finger on the pulse.

He swung away. *No, not Ellie's pulse.* Although if she didn't get here soon he might have to throttle her.

He was a busy man. He didn't have time to… He checked his watch. Nearly nine-fifteen. …Didn't have time to *waste*.

At ten o'clock he rang Joanie to tell her he'd been detained, that he'd phone again when he was on his way.

Responsibility. They'd talked about it. Ellie had worked two days and been on time. Perhaps that was her limit. He tapped in her phone number. Swore when her phone was switched off. She had no answering service so he couldn't leave a voice message.

He paced to the window, glared at the front gate. When she arrived he'd tell her his expectations: While he was here, he preferred—wanted—her to keep regular hours… Damn, why wait until she'd arrived? He'd go inform her himself. That way he could drive her here if she was running late.

A short time later he parked and stared up at her sorry-looking apartment building. Daylight showed the dull facade in all its unspectacular glory. Grey peeling paintwork. Dusty windows.

He climbed out of his car and walked to the door. In this instance he was relieved it wasn't a coded entry—except that anyone could walk in off the street. He took the stairs two at a time and followed a dingy passage until he found apartment number four, then knocked on the door.

No answer. Impatience snapped at him; he barely waited before knocking again, louder, longer. 'Ellie, are you in there?'

A scruffy-looking sort in a grey hooded jacket with straggly blond hair and teenage fuzz above his upper lip exited an apartment down the hall. Mid- to late teens, Matt figured. The odour of sweat and dirty sneakers preceded the guy as he approached.

Matt's nostrils flared in distaste. But Ellie had no choice; she couldn't afford anything better. Matt understood that all too well.

'She ain't left yet,' Scruffy said as he passed Matt.

He studied the youth through narrowed eyes. 'And you'd know this how?'

Scruffy popped a wad of chewing gum in his mouth. 'See everyone from my living room window. You dropped her off last night. Night before too. Black Ford, right?'

A twinge of concern jolted through Matt. 'Do you watch everyone's comings and goings?'

'Pretty much,' he said cheerfully. 'Ain't safe round here. It's just me and Mum, and she's in a wheelchair, so I keep an eye out.'

'And you are?'

'Toby.' He stuck his hands in the pockets of his hoodie. 'You Ellie's new boyfriend?'

'I'm... Yes,' Matt decided. One could never be too careful and any woman living alone was always a potential target, even if Toby seemed harmless enough. 'My name's Matt. I'll see you around.'

'Okay. See ya.' Toby hunched into his hoodie and headed to the stairwell.

Matt resumed knocking. 'Ellie, I know you're in there. Answer the door.' Finally he heard a muffled sound and the door cracked open. Her face was only partially visible and what he could see didn't look good.

'What are you doing here?' She sniffed, dug a tissue from the pocket of her dressing gown, held it to her nose.

No wonder she hadn't turned up. 'You're ill,' he said unnecessarily. 'You should have phoned me.' He pushed the door wider, took in the dark circles beneath her glassy eyes before closing the door behind him.

'Why?' She turned away and headed over the worn linoleum floor towards her bed. She wore flannelette pyjamas under her robe, he noticed, and fluffy pink slippers.

'To let me know you weren't coming in...' His voice was tight and clipped to his own ears. He saw the way her shoulders drooped and softened it with, 'To let me know if you need anything.' He glanced about him at the tiny studio apartment. The place was basic at best. And colder than an antarctic winter.

'On my day off?'

'Your day off?'

'I don't work Thursdays. I told you that at our *interview*.' Stepping out of her slippers, she crawled onto the bed, dragging the covers over her. 'So, if there's nothing else... Pull the door shut behind you on your way out.'

Even with his jacket on, his skin goose-bumped beneath his cashmere jumper. 'Don't you have heating?'

'It's broken down,' she mumbled.

'I can't leave you here like this.'

'Sure you can. Don't you have appointments to keep? Five-star hotels to frequent?' A hand appeared from beneath the quilt to grab another tissue.

Five-star hotels? 'What are you talking about?' He crossed the room, stared down at her, shook his questions away. 'Forget appointments, forget work. You shouldn't be on your own and this place is an icebox. You're coming home with me.'

CHAPTER SIX

'No.' HER reply was razor sharp.

'I don't want to argue with you, Ellie.'

'Good.' A beat of silence. 'I'm better off here. If I can sleep it off today, I'll be right for work tomorrow.'

He lowered himself to the edge of the bed, his shoe skittering against something as he sat. He looked down…

His business card. Crumpled. By one very tight, very deliberate fist, if he guessed correctly. He picked it up, lowered the quilt so he could see her face and waved it in front of her. 'I must've made a good impression Saturday night.'

Her eyes flicked open, then widened as she realised. 'Oh.' She blinked up at him. 'How did that get there?'

He felt a corner of his mouth tip up. 'You didn't throw it out.' He smoothed it out, tapped it against his chin. 'This tells me something, Ellie.'

Her eyes slid shut again. 'It tells you I'm environmentally aware, that I was waiting for the paper recycling day to come round.'

'Yeah. Right.' He slipped it beneath her pillow with a smile she didn't see.

He glanced about the apartment. Her fridge was covered in kids' paintings held in place by frog magnets. 'Whose artwork?'

'I volunteer at a homework centre for disadvantaged kids,' she mumbled into her pillow.

A volunteer? She was more than he'd given her credit for and something deeper stirred inside him. Willing the somewhat disturbing feeling away, his gaze landed on a small but familiar figurine on the scarred night stand.

He looked back at Ellie, her eyelashes resting on pale cheeks, then picked it up, rolled it between his palms. 'Where did you get this?'

Her eyes opened halfway. 'Belle gave it to me. She said everyone needs a guardian angel.'

Matt knew it wasn't a simple trinket. It was one of a kind, according to Belle. She'd bought it in Venice a few years back and paid a fortune in tourist dollars for it. Did Ellie know its true value?

He folded the quilt back and tucked the edge beneath her chin. 'Guardian angels won't cut it today. You can sleep in Belle's guest room.'

'No.'

He tightened his jaw. 'I can carry you downstairs in your pyjamas and put you in the car myself or you can get dressed first—your choice. But you're coming with me in five minutes.'

'I'm staying here. I'm going to try to sleep. *Here*. Thanks for your offer, now go away.'

He pushed up. So be it. He found an empty supermarket bag, then scouted the room for something she could wear later—a black tracksuit sprawled over a chair and a pair of sneakers with socks spilling out nearby. 'Four minutes.' He opened drawers till he found underwear.

Behind him, he heard her gasp. 'You are *so not* touching my—'

'Think again, honey.' He pulled out a filmy white bra and panties, tossed them in the bag. Added a pair of socks.

Ellie's eyes narrowed to slits as she watched Matt's broad-shouldered shape disappear into her tiny bathroom. Her heart thudded erratically against the mattress. She pushed the tissue against her lips to prevent a whimper when she heard the clatter of bottles being scooped up. Squeezing her eyes shut, she willed him to leave. She was an independent woman. Had to be. If she refused to move, made it obvious she didn't want his assistance, didn't *need* it, he'd respect that. He'd—

Her eyes snapped open again when the quilt's warmth vanished. A tide of cold air and defeat washed over her as she gazed up at one determined man. Mouth resolute. Jaw squared, brow furrowed. Her bag of stuff on his arm.

A man accustomed to having his demands met.

Well, she had news for him. 'Listen, I...' His dark eyes challenged hers and she felt her words drain away with her resolve.

'Since you're obviously not going to cooperate—' he continued, sliding his hands beneath her armpits '—why wait the extra two minutes?'

As he dragged her upright, she saw the glint in his eyes and her heart leapt with a contrary thrill in her chest. 'You wouldn't...'

The glint remained as he slid her slippers onto her feet. He tightened the sash on her dressing gown, fastened the top button of her pyjamas. 'Yes, Ellie, I would.' Then scooping her up, he swung her into his arms.

His jumper tickled her nose, his hold was so tight the only air she could breathe was full of his scent. She kicked—uselessly—since her legs hit nothing but air. 'Put. Me. Down.' Her futile demand was muffled against his chest.

'Not until we reach the car.' His voice rumbled against her ear. She felt herself being carried across the room. He passed the kitchen table, dumped her handbag on her lap.

'This is crazy. I'm not ill. I have a cold, that's all.'

He gave her a disbelieving look. 'Keys?'

She thought about refusing to tell him, but she doubted it would make any difference, and being locked out wasn't a sensible idea either because she was *coming back tonight* if she had to walk it. 'On the hook by the door.'

Grabbing them on the way, he stepped into the hallway and pulled the door shut behind him. The click echoed in the dimness. He started down the stairs and she had no choice but to hang on and let him do his macho-hero thing.

His car was parked right out front. She flopped down in the seat with a scowl, but couldn't help sighing at the sun's warmth through the windscreen.

Sniffing, she turned her head away so she wouldn't have to look at him when he climbed in and set the car in motion. Lucky for her, she wasn't looking for a man in her life. And even if she was, it was lucky Matt McGregor was far too domineering.

Because it meant she could relegate him to the back of her mind and only deal with him when it was absolutely necessary. Like now, unfortunately.

She watched the streetscape change from concrete and retail to the upscale mansions behind hedges and greenery as they neared Belle's place.

She frowned. So why did her insides still insist on turning themselves about when she thought of him? And how could she help thinking about him when she couldn't seem to avoid him? Like this morning. How many darn times had he felt that manly need to come to her assistance?

She didn't need him or his help.

Her inconvenient sneeze prompted a tissue to appear in front of her face. She took it with a scowl and a muttered, 'Thanks.' She was *not* going to be that weak, needy, ditzy woman he seemed to think she was.

'Asking for help isn't a sign of weakness, Ellie.'

She swiped her nose, then stared at him. Did the man read her thoughts now? 'I *didn't* ask.'

His face was in profile; his eyes were hidden behind his sunglasses. 'Because you *misplaced* my business card and didn't know how to contact me?'

'Because I...' She let her head fall back and rolled her eyes up to the car's interior light. 'I have Belle's home number. If I'd needed to, I could've contacted you.'

'And if I'd left earlier for the office, as I'd intended?'

'Why *didn't* you leave earlier—and why are we having this conversation?'

The moment the car came to a halt near the front porch, she swung the door open. Her dressing gown flapped around her ankles in the wind as she walked up the path. How she must look—bed hair and flannel pyjamas and handbag. Yesterday's make-up. Rudolph's red nose and it wasn't even Christmas. She pressed her lips together. She hadn't even cleaned her teeth this morning.

He unlocked the door and ushered her inside. 'Go on up. Belle always leaves the bed made in case of unexpected visitors,' he told her, handing her the supermarket bag. 'I'll bring you a cup of lemon tea before I leave.'

She stared at him. Did he not know when to stop? And yet...someone doing something nice for her, looking after her, warmed her insides like Gran's bread-and-butter pudding.

His brow rose. 'Unless you want me to carry you again?'

She shook her head and walked towards the staircase.

Ten minutes later Matt appeared with the promised tray of lemon tea, one of Belle's delicate dishes arranged with sticks of carrot, cheese, olives and celery and an unopened packet of her favourite chocolate biscuits. He set it on the little doily-covered table beside the bed. 'Help yourself to anything in the fridge. Get some sleep. I'll be back by teatime.'

'Thanks. I...appreciate it.'

He reached for her hand and for a furious pulse-beat she thought he was going to bring it to his lips, but he pulled out a pen and wrote a string of numbers on the inside of her wrist.

'If you need me,' he told her.

And just like that her whole body melted at the subconscious message those words conveyed. She closed her eyes. 'I'll be all right.'

When Ellie woke, her stuffy head had cleared somewhat and her throat was a little better, courtesy of the cold-and-flu medication Matt had included on the tray.

Early-winter gloom had plunged the room into semidarkness, but rather than the dank chill of her apartment, the afternoon sunshine's warmth still lingered in the room, the fragrance of fresh linen filled the air.

And for a moment she was a little girl again, in her own bedroom with the fairyland wallpaper and chintz curtains. A time when she'd been too young to understand the meaning of loss, or to appreciate the value of family.

Snuggling deeper into the lavender-scented sheets, she indulged in those long-forgotten memories of safety and warmth, love. All the more precious because once upon a time this home had belonged to her grandfather's family.

As she shifted position, she caught sight of Matt's mobile number on her wrist. Heat flooded through her when she remembered the feel of his hand brushing her arm as he'd penned the numbers.

And another thought occurred to her. Was it only the history of the house or was Matt also partially responsible for bringing all these feelings to the surface?

She'd seen a different side to him over the past couple of days. He might be hot, but whether she wanted to admit it or not, there was a comfortable warmth there too. A warmth that had nothing to do with sexuality and everything to do with the kind of man he was. The kind that made you want to cuddle right up and share…what? Your deepest secrets? Hopes and fears?

How could she reconcile that with the sexy Matt who made her want to cuddle up and share a whole lot more than confidences?

Matt was also a take-charge kind of guy. How would that translate in the bedroom? she wondered, her mind straying into forbidden territory. Would he expect to make all the moves? Or did he like to lie back sometimes and let a woman do the work? Her body tingled, grew languid at the new and dangerous direction her thoughts had taken.

Until she remembered that he'd had a date last night. The feeling seeped out of her, leaving a cold empty space in the pit of her stomach. Probably someone like Yasmine from the office. Tall, career-oriented, killer body, long smooth *straight* hair. Unlike her own flyaway frizz that hadn't seen a pair of straighteners in the past forty-eight hours.

She needed to ignore that warm cosy feeling that kept creeping up on her whenever she thought of Matt's caring side. She needed to ignore those hot forbidden fantasies that sprang to life whenever he looked at her.

He wasn't in Melbourne for long, she reminded herself. She only had to survive a few more days, and in the meantime she'd give him no reason to think she was interested in pursuing what they'd started any further.

So it wouldn't be a problem when he left.

And she'd go back to her life the way she preferred it. No-one with promises they didn't keep, no unrealistic expectations, no broken heart.

Alone.

Safe.

* * *

The house was in darkness when Matt let himself in around 6:00 p.m. He headed straight for the guest room, a strange anticipation twirling through him like streamers at Sydney's Mardi Gras parade.

A glimmer of light slanted across the hallway. Her door remained partially open as he'd left it. The lamp on the night stand, dimmed to its lowest setting, cast subtle shadows over Ellie. He'd intended asking her what she fancied eating but quickly decided she needed sleep more than sustenance.

Her hair formed a curly halo around her face; long lashes rested on porcelain cheeks. The top button of her pyjamas had slipped undone, revealing the gold locket she always wore nestled in her dusky cleavage. Beautiful.

And vulnerable.

He should step back, give her privacy, but his eyes refused to look away. His feet held fast and his hand tightened around the edge of the door.

He wanted to cross the room, brush his hand over her hair and enjoy its texture. To skim her cheek, lay his lips on hers and reacquaint himself with her taste.

He imagined her waking to his touch. Amethyst eyes blinking up at him, turning dark as he slid his palms between flannel and warm skin. Then he'd soothe that innate caution she seemed to have with soft words, softer kisses. His fingers itched and his mouth watered.

He dragged his gaze away from the bed to the darkened window while his thoughts drifted back to yesterday. She wasn't as carefree and irresponsible as she'd initially have had him believe. And perhaps she wasn't the type of woman he could easily walk away from without it playing on his conscience.

He'd need to make it clear that there was no chance of anything serious developing between them. He didn't do long-term. He'd been unable to give Angela the happy-ever-after marriage and children because long-term commitment didn't work—he'd been witness to that too many times to count. He knew Belle's heart had been broken when the man she'd loved had walked away, even though she'd never discussed the details.

And the innocent kids when two people decided they'd had enough—where the hell did that leave them? Ellie's father. His own mother. He didn't want to hurt Ellie the same way.

Didn't mean he wanted her in his bed any less. As soon as she'd recovered, he told himself.

The following morning Matt stood at the kitchen window watching the rain while he scooped up cereal, racking his brains for a reason other than gardening to keep Ellie here for the day. Assuming she was well enough. Hoping she was recovered because having her sleep so near that he could practically hear her breathing was playing havoc with his libido.

Ellie appeared in the doorway, already showered and dressed in her tracksuit. Her complexion was pale, her nose still red, but other than that, she looked...like Ellie.

He couldn't believe the way her presence lifted the kitchen's ambience. And his mood. 'Good morning.' He hefted the coffeepot. 'You'd be feeling like a coffee, I imagine?'

'Hi. Yes. Please.' She walked a few steps, hesitated. 'I didn't mean to sleep all night. Sorry if I inconvenienced you in any way. I intended going home.'

'I hardly knew you were here.' Yeah, right. He'd not been able to think of anything else. For most of the night he'd been uncomfortably awake and aware that she'd been a few quick steps down the hall. He set a mug of coffee on the kitchen table. 'How are you feeling this morning?'

'Much better, thanks.'

'I'll let you know now, I don't expect you to work in the rain.'

'Oh. Good.' She picked up the mug but remained standing. 'So, I…'

'So, I…'

Both spoke at the same time. She raised her mug at him. 'Yes?'

'I was going to say if you'd like to work today and you're feeling up to it, I've got an indoor job for you.'

'Oh?' Relief crossed her expression. 'Great. I could do with the extra money.'

'The downstairs windows could do with a wash. I'm sure Belle would appreciate it.'

She smiled. 'Just show me where the gear is, point me in the right direction and I'll get started.'

'No rush. Finish your coffee while I make you some breakfast.'

'You don't have to go to all that trouble, the caffeine hit's fine.'

'Belle would skin me alive if I forced you to work on an empty stomach. How does scrambled egg sound?'

'Wonderful, but I can do it if you need to be some-where.…'

'I've got a luncheon appointment but that's hours away. Why don't you find what you need in the laundry and set up while I cook?'

Ellie set to work as soon as she'd eaten the meal Matt had prepared for her, which had been every bit as tasty as she'd expected. To her relief, he didn't sit with her while she ate because a business call came through requiring his attention.

She started in the dining and living rooms, admiring the exquisite cream, rose and jade furnishings against the dark antique furniture as she set up the stepladder and got to work.

Next she chose a cosy little room down the hall which would catch the afternoon sun and give hours of pleasure on a cold winter's day. Bookcases overloaded with classics lined one wall.

Another shelf was crammed with fifties memorabilia. A selection of old vinyl 45s sat atop a small record player. Bill Haley's 'Rock around the Clock,' Pat Boone's 'Love Letters in the Sand.' The Platters, Elvis.

A photo album caught Ellie's eye. On the front was a black-and-white image of a teenage Belle. Ellie recognised the shape of her face, the wide eyes and broad cheekbones. But the hair was a surprise—pulled back in a curly ponytail, not unlike her own unruly locks. She was dressed in a full-skirted gingham-checked dress cinched at the waist with a wide belt and wore a heart-shaped locket around her neck.

Ellie's fingers tangled in the slim chain of her own locket which had belonged to her mother. A tingle danced over her nape, as if someone had stroked a finger down her spine.

Shaking the sensation away, she set the album back in place. But for just a heartbeat or two she'd been mesmerised by the image and a strange feeling that she was missing a piece of a puzzle.

CHAPTER SEVEN

A SHORT time later she was halfway up the stepladder when Matt appeared to inform her he was leaving. He wore a white shirt, silver-grey silk tie, dark trousers and a chocolate-brown suede jacket. Smelling fresh and masculine and entirely too sexy to be heading out to anything remotely concerned with business.

But then…he hadn't mentioned *business*, had he? Only that he had a luncheon appointment. Which was open to all manner of interpretation.

Something slithered through Ellie's belly and coiled tight around the top of her already stuffy chest, making it hard to breathe. Something that felt horribly, unimaginably like… possessiveness. Her fingers tightened on her little bucket of water, her other hand clutched the top rung of the ladder. *No.* It was *not* that. No way.

She saw his brows pull down. 'Are you okay?'

And before she could blink he'd crossed the room and was beside her, his face too close, his hands reaching for her shoulders. With Ellie on the ladder, they were the same height. His eyes almost lined up with hers. His mouth was… too close.

'You startled me, damn you.' *Damn his luncheon date. And damn her dumb reaction.* She jerked away from his touch.

A few drops of water splashed out of the bucket and onto his shirt.

'Ah…'

'Yes, *ah*.' He took the bucket from her nerveless fingers, set it down out of harm's way, then straightened to face her.

Biting her lip, she stared at the damp splotch, but then her traitorous gaze shifted to the dark hairs barely visible beneath the fine textured fabric. To his neck, and the pinpricks of newly shaved stubble. His Adam's apple.

She sucked in a breath, bringing the scent of his aftershave with it, and she forgot all about luncheon dates and being snippy.

She was too busy being turned on.

An image of her loosening his tie, slipping his buttons undone and spreading his shirt open, sliding her hands between fabric and olive skin danced behind her eyes. Setting her mouth to that masculine throat…

Swallowing hard, she dragged her eyes away…and up…to meet a pair of dark assessing eyes. 'Sorry—' she lifted one finger of her free hand '—about the shirt.'

He leaned nearer. She could see flecks of hazel in his dark irises. A tiny bald patch in his left eyebrow.

'What are you going to do about it?' His breath whispered against her mouth, a current of energy arcing between them.

'Um, I have a dry cloth somewhere.…' She didn't try to find it. Sparks. She was sure there must be sparks.

'Won't help.' He slid his free hand over her shoulder, traced a line over her shoulderblade. Used the move to draw her closer. She could feel his masculine heat and strength radiating off him. 'Ellie?'

Her legs threatened to give way. They weren't even touching but his lips were heating hers, making the blood rush to

her cheeks, sending those sparks sizzling through her blood.
'Yes?'

'Kiss me.'

Her breath stalled in her throat. 'What?'

His deep chuckle vibrated along her bones. 'You know how
it goes. You put your lips on mine and I…reciprocate.'

'I'm working. And it's business hours.' But, oh, the temptation. It tingled on her lips, her tongue. Tap-danced over her
skin and twisted through her limbs.

'I won't tell the boss.' He leaned in, lips puckered. 'Your
call, Ellie. You're in the driver's seat with this one.'

She huffed, 'Fine, then, if it'll get you to leave quicker,'
and leaned in to meet him.

Hah. From the instant their lips touched, any notion that she
held the upper hand was whipped away by a blast of astonish-
ing masculine know-how. She should have known better with
a man like Matt McGregor. In a response that screamed need,
Ellie relinquished that control. She wanted more—craved it
as his hands cruised up and down her spine, as he tilted his
head for better access.

Her mouth fell open beneath his. She tasted temptation and
desire—his and hers. Heard both in the soft throaty sounds
scrambling up her throat. Felt it in the heavy hardness that
rocked against her belly as his hand slid over the curve of her
buttocks and tilted her toward him.

It should have been enough, this fleeting sensory indulgence; temporary was all she knew he was looking for. It
should have been enough for her too.

But he lifted a hand to cup her jaw as if he held antique
china, and the determination behind her resolve melted like
frost on grass on a bright winter morning. This man was…
more. Dangerously more.

Because he drew emotions from her that she'd learned
to keep buried down deep, that she no longer wanted to

acknowledge. The warm feeling of being wanted, valued as a person. Cherished, even, for who she was. She'd become an expert at holding that part of herself back until Matt McGregor had strolled into her life. And it came at a price. Vulnerability.

She yanked herself out of his hold. Gripped the ladder with both hands. Her arms felt leaden, her muscles had turned to water. And it was only marginally comforting to see that he was as breathless as she. That his eyes blazed with the same heat she was sure hers signalled.

But his interest was skin deep. And that heat would cool soon enough, she knew. It always did. Turning away, she reached for the cloth she'd left on top of the ladder. 'You'll be late for your luncheon appointment.'

Who he was meeting was none of her concern. They'd kissed. So what? It didn't make them an item. Permanent playboy and gardener did not a couple make.

'Have dinner with me tonight.'

His deeper-than-midnight voice had her turning back to look at him. 'Dinner?'

He shrugged. 'Why not? It's after-hours. There's a new Moroccan restaurant not far away I've been wanting to try. Or we can do something else, if you'd prefer....'

'Dinner's good,' she said quickly. Dinner was probably the lesser of two evils. The way he'd said 'something else' sounded decidedly risky if the way her pulse had tripped was any indication.

'I'll make a booking.' He passed her the bucket of water. 'I'm calling by the office after lunch so I'll pick you up from your place around 6:00 p.m.'

'Umm,' she murmured, her mind all over the place. 'Oh— It's Friday.'

'Is that a problem?'

'I'm at the homework centre Friday afternoons. I'm there till six. Never mind about dinner, another—'

'We'll make it seven. Where's the centre?'

'In that old church building with the peppercorn tree out front a couple of blocks from my place, but—'

'Okay. I'll see you later.'

Ellie worked furiously for the next few hours, stopping only to put together a sandwich while she stressed about the up-coming evening. It felt strange helping herself to the contents of Belle's fridge, but what choice did she have? She'd been practically kidnapped here.

Matt was weakening her resolve not to get involved, that's what he was doing. Breaking down her defences with serious acts of gallantry, seducing her with searing hot looks and that deep velvet voice.

She plunked her backside on the bottom rung of the ladder. No fancy wine—she'd stick to mineral water. Just because she didn't intend getting involved—with anyone—didn't mean she couldn't enjoy some company, and he was going to turn up at seven o'clock in any case.

Next problem—what to wear? Her one and only black dress? She frowned. It might give him the impression she'd dressed up especially for him. So jeans and T-shirt with her black jacket for warmth.

Decision made, she packed the belongings she'd brought with her to Belle's and headed off for the kid's centre.

'Okay, crew, who wants to help plant the pansies?'

A chorus of 'Me, me, me' chimed around Ellie as the kids clustered eagerly about her.

'Okay, here we go.' She handed out the punnets she'd paid for herself. 'Careful, there's plenty for everyone.'

Ellie had established a garden plot at the back of the

building with the help of half a dozen interested kids. They'd
planned what they wanted as a team, designed the plot and
purchased the plants, giving them pride and ownership. An
older girl, Jenny, was helping Wayne to separate parsley seedlings and plant them into prepared holes.

But Brandon was having none of it. He lounged on the side-
line, all skinny limbs and attitude, but Ellie knew he wanted
to join in, and her heart went out to him. She knew he lived
with a father who didn't give two hoots. If she only knew how
to involve him.

'How about hunting for wildlife, then?'

Ellie's head swivelled at the sound of Matt's voice behind
her. He gave her a quick look and a murmured, 'I've cleared
it with the boss inside,' then approached Brandon and squat-
ted beside him, holding a box. He was still wearing the suit
jacket he'd left home in earlier.

'There's no wildlife here,' Brandon scoffed, rolling his eyes.
The corner of his mouth curled…as if a grown man could be
so dumb.

'Sure there is. Slimy snails and creepy crawlies. Huge fat
spiders with hairy legs, if you know where to look. Want to
help me find them?'

'Nope.'

'Okay… By the way, my name's Matt and I'm a friend of
Ellie's.' He produced a couple of magnifying glasses from
the box. 'Ever watched the forensic scientists on those crime
scene investigation programs on TV?'

Brandon gave him a cursory glance. 'We don't have a TV.'
He scuffed a worn sneaker along the ground. 'But I've seen
it on Nan's.'

'Well, you'll know that sometimes they look for insects
and stuff to help solve a crime scene. I'm going to have a look
round here and see what I can find. I need an assistant with
good investigative skills to help me. How about it?'

And just like that, Matt had Brandon eating out of his hand.

Ellie watched them scour the seemingly lifeless asphalted area a few moments later. Watched their heads bent close together as they studied something in the weeds along the perimeter. Who'd have thought the man would have a way with kids? Yet she knew nothing of his past or how he'd come to live with Belle, except that the memories still haunted him.

A short time later she saw the pair of them sitting on a log seat away from the rest of the kids. This time Brandon was doing the talking, Matt was listening. Nodding. Sharing. And Ellie's heart rolled over like a giant tumbleweed in her chest.

'…And we want to extend the rear of the building into a music-cum-dance-cum-drama room,' Ellie said as they exited the centre and walked towards Matt's car. She'd given him a tour of the place and told him all about the grand albeit pie-in-the-sky plans they had. 'And if we had the finances we'd employ artists and musicians and offer a breakfast program. These kids need all that and more.'

'You're really passionate about it, aren't you?'

A warm feeling that he understood burrowed through her. 'You'd better believe it. Thanks for your help with Brandon. He's a tough little nut to crack.'

Matt pulled out his car key, pressed the remote. 'Next time I come, I'll bring my microscope.'

She stared at him over the top of the car. 'You'd come again?'

'Sure.' He grinned at her. 'Why should you get to have all the fun?'

Ellie nearly melted right there. He liked kids. Oh, dear. She was a goner.

CHAPTER EIGHT

DARKNESS was already swallowing what little day was left when Matt dropped her outside her apartment building to change for dinner. The rain clouds had blown away, leaving a hard indigo sky. The aroma of damp bitumen and a charcoal grill somewhere hung on the still air.

A car cruised the street, slowing as it neared. Ellie tugged her tracksuit jacket a little higher. She never let thoughts of murder and mayhem bother her. If she did, she'd never go anywhere. But she breathed a little easier when it passed by.

Climbing the stairs in the dimness—the darn stairwell light hadn't been replaced for three weeks—she dug in her pocket for her keys. Her thoughts were focused on a quick shower in her draughty bathroom, a little make-up…

But rational thought evaporated when she lifted her hand to put her key to the lock. *Splintered wood.* Her whole body tightened and her blood drained into her legs.

While she'd been overnighting at Belle's place someone had intruded on her sanctuary. The one place she should be able to feel safe. How long she stood there she didn't know—listening for noises from within, hearing only her heartbeat pounding in her ears.

Gradually she became aware of other sounds. Down the hall the reassuring sound of Mrs Larson's TV and, intermittently, Toby's voice. Outside, city sounds. Inside…silence.

Scarcely aware that she was holding her breath, she reached out, fingers touching the scarred wood. The door opened with a light push. Keeping her gaze dead ahead, she felt for the switch to her left. Light flooded the room and spilled into the bathroom beyond. Empty. The one advantage to having a studio apartment was the ability to see everything in a single glance, she thought grimly, stepping inside and pushing the door closed behind her.

The inspection didn't take long. Then she sat on her bed and started to laugh, a touch hysterically. The laugh was on them—financially challenged Ellie Rose had nothing of value to steal. But they'd obviously taken exception to the time and effort they'd wasted and left the contents of her fridge strewn over the floor.

She realised her hands were shaking and her throat was dry. Someone had touched her things, breathed the same air, invaded her space. Chills crawled over her flesh and down her spine. Grabbing her quilt, she tugged it around her, then almost as quickly pushed it away—irrational, but it felt dirty somehow and a chill shuddered down her spine. What if whoever-it-was had touched it? She felt violated and alone.

Jerking up, she paced to the kitchen sink, adrenaline and anger pumping through her body.

Matt found her crouched by the refrigerator, mopping up the mess with a kitchen sponge. The fact that her door was open and damaged and that she hadn't answered his knock had struck him with fear like he'd never experienced. A primitive instinct to protect what was his drummed through his body. 'Ellie.'

She jolted at the sound of his voice, then froze for a second like a trapped animal. 'I'm... Okay.' She resumed her task with a choked attempt at a laugh. 'The scumbag hung around here long enough to drink my last can of Coke.'

Crouching down beside her, he took the sponge from her fingers. 'Leave it, Ellie.'

'I have to clean this mess.'

'No. You don't. I'll have a cleaning service come in tomorrow.'

'I need to keep busy.' She waved a hand. 'Nervous energy and all that.'

He tipped her chin up, hating the naked distress he saw written all over her face. 'Busy, hmm?' He smiled into her eyes, taking his time about it. 'I can help you with that.' He kept his voice light, teasing even, but inside...inside he wanted to punch the living daylights out of the low-life who'd done this to her.

He rose, pulling her up with him, his hands beneath her elbows to steady her. 'Did they take anything?'

'I don't think so.'

'Have you rung the cops?'

'No.'

'I'll do it now, then.' He smoothed his hands down her back, drawing her closer. 'It's going to be all right, Ellie. I'm here.'

The last words didn't surprise him, but the emotions they invoked did. Feeling the fragility of her bones beneath his hands and that tiny slender frame against his...it drew up a well of tenderness he'd not known existed. He wanted to go on holding her and— *Protect what was his?*

His whole body tightened. Where the hell had that come from? He'd seen the broken lock and Ellie on the floor and had simply reacted. He was no knight in shining armour.

Loosening his hold, he stepped back, uneasy with the emotions she'd conjured in him. Assured himself it was a momentary thing. She'd proclaimed herself an independent woman; she had no need for such masculine displays of chivalry.

'I can manage,' she said, backing up at the same time.

As if she'd read his thoughts. But beneath that *I-don't-need-you-to-take-care-of-me* facade he could see the little-girl-lost lurking in her eyes and he had to clench his fists at his sides so as not to reach for her again. If he touched her, he might give her more than she was willing to accept. More than he was willing to give.

Swinging away, he paced to the other side of the room. 'I'll double-check everything's okay—you might have missed something. I'll look into finding you alternative accommodation tomorrow.'

'But I don't have the finances to—'

'Don't worry about that now.' He waved a hand. 'I'll arrange something. I know people. There are studio apartments near the university. Safe and clean. It'll be fine, trust me. I'll make those calls, then we'll get something to eat. Takeaway's probably best under the circumstances.'

'Something hot with a bite to it,' she said, swiping at her damp-kneed sweatpants with a muttered curse. 'Beef vindaloo with teeth.'

Over the next twenty minutes he rang the police, organised a cleaning service and someone to fix the door and add extra security—no way was he waiting around for some absent landlord—while Ellie showered and changed.

A couple of hours and a police report later, they were in the car on the way back to Belle's place with Ellie's requested Indian takeaway.

How had she gone from living in relative comfort as a child to...this? 'You don't have to answer this, Ellie,' he said as the car idled at an intersection. 'But wasn't there some sort of inheritance when your mum passed away?'

She was silent a moment and he thought she wasn't going to answer. Finally she said, 'My family invested in a company that went bust. They lost a substantial amount of their wealth only months before the accident.'

'That's tough.' Damn, he should have kept his mouth shut. As the lights changed, he set the car in motion again. 'Forget I asked.'

'I don't mind.' From the corner of his eye he saw her chin lift. 'I'm not ashamed.'

'Nor should you be.'

'Mum left what she had to my father. When Dad walked out on us, she obviously gave no thought to changing her will, which she'd made before I was even born. I only learned about it when I was old enough to understand.'

So that's why Ellie's father had turned up after her mother's death—not out of any sense of parental duty but because he thought he'd come into wealth. Matt's lip curled in disgust. 'What about his family?' he asked. 'Your paternal grandparents? Couldn't they help?'

'Both dead, back in England. He emigrated here on his own. Of course he used what money there was to keep us together,' Ellie hurried on. Seemed she was determined to defend him. 'Even though we moved around a lot, we lived in nice places, ate at the best restaurants. But he was a gambler,' she finished quietly.

Ah. It didn't take a PhD to figure the man had left his daughter again when the money had run out. 'Didn't the courts make provisions for you as her daughter?'

'They did. It was kept in trust for me until I turned eighteen....'

Something in her voice alerted him, pushed him to say, 'Let me guess, your father turned up.'

She didn't reply.

He shook his head. 'Ellie, Ellie. Don't you know feeding a gambling problem only makes it worse?'

'He said he'd changed. He's my father. The only family I have left.'

Her tone tugged at something deep down inside him. 'He used that against you—you know that, don't you?'

He could feel the pain his words caused across the space between them and felt like a jerk, but she said, 'I insisted he use it to get help. And at least I used some of it to finance most of my horticultural course.'

'I didn't mean to insult you.'

'I know. It's just that people like you don't have a clue about people like me.'

He let it pass. *You don't want to talk about yourself, Matt—don't bring it up.*

They turned into the driveway; the gates swung open, revealing the magnificent home in all its eccentric splendour. Proclaiming wealth from the tip of its spired turret to the landscaped front garden with its statues, ponds and carefully tended topiary.

He knew how it must look, but Ellie had no idea how much they had in common.

Matt switched on the TV and left Ellie in the lounge room while he found plates and set their meal out on the table.

Then since they weren't eating out, he headed upstairs to change into something casual. A shadow of movement alerted him as he passed Belle's room. He saw Ellie place Belle's angel on the night stand.

'Ellie?'

She jerked at his voice and spun to face him. 'Don't sneak up on me like that. I'm jittery enough as it is.'

He stepped into the room, intrigued. 'Why would you return a gift?'

She turned her attention back to the angel, caressed it. 'It's safer here. Thank you. For helping me out. And for this afternoon with the kids.'

She looked over then, and smiled at him—just a hint but,

ah, God, it was as if the sun came out. He wanted to pull her close, kiss away the demons he saw in her eyes, but that special kind of intimacy was more than he had in him to give. He didn't want to get emotionally involved. For her sake as well as his own. He turned away. 'Anyone would do the same. Let's go put a dent in that curry.'

They sat down to tandoori chicken and beef vindaloo with rice, servings of crisp pappadums, cool cucumber raita and tangy mango chutney. Ellie attacked her meal with a vengeance which appeared to be borne of anger rather than hunger.

Finding your apartment ransacked was a rotten end to anyone's day. He picked up his glass, took a few mouthfuls of water—she'd refused his suggestion of wine so he'd opted out too—and watched her. The way her lips closed over the spoon, lightly glossed with oil. Her fingers, slender with short, unpolished nails.

He could almost feel those fingers drifting over him in pleasure, clutching at him in passion. He shifted uncomfortably on his chair. In the silence he could almost hear his own blood rushing through his veins and making his jeans two sizes too tight.

Timing again.

The best he could do was to take her mind off her troubles and his mind off his libido. 'What do you do when you're feeling down, Ellie?'

'I'm not down, just angry.' She stabbed a cube of beef, shoved it in her mouth and chewed vigorously.

'So what do you do when you're angry?'

'Run.' A small smile lifted the edges of her mouth. 'Not the running-away quitting kind of running, the simple mind-clearing act of pushing one's self to the limit. That nervous energy I mentioned? I channel it. If there was a beach nearby that's what I'd do. With the wind on my face and the sound of surf in my ears. I'd run until I couldn't run another step, then I'd stand on a cliff and watch the waves roll in. And pray for a storm.'

He set his glass down, laid his hands on the table. 'How about now?'

Ellie's brow pleated. 'It's hardly beach weather.'

'Does that stop you?'

'Well, no…'

He leaned back and watched her. 'Ever ridden a motorbike?'

'No.'

'There's nothing like it. Hitting the bitumen, outriding your problems. Ride till you come to the end of the road. Same rush, same result. I have an idea.' He rose, skirted the table and reached for her hand, tugged her up, then headed for the door.

'Wait up, where are we going?'

He turned to her and grinned. 'My place.'

'*Your* place?' Ellie stared at those beguiling brown eyes while her heart thudded loud and strong against her ribs. 'I thought you lived here when you come to Melbourne.'

'Nope. My place is down the coast a bit along the Great Ocean Road. Lorne has the best view in the world.'

'But Lorne's a couple of hours' drive away.'

'Less if the traffic's light. It's a clear night. What better way to dust off the cobwebs and get that adrenaline pumping?'

'Hang on…' A frisson of something like excitement inextricably bound with alarm zipped down her spine. 'A motorbike was mentioned. You're going to ride there?'

'No, *we're* going to ride there.' When she just stared at him while that adrenaline geysered up and churned with her dinner, he smiled. 'Don't worry, Ellie. I've got two helmets and I don't take risks.'

'But it's already nearly ten o'clock.' She did *not* add that

10:00 p.m. was her routine bedtime. Although tonight she wasn't anywhere near ready to sleep.

His eyes darkened and his voice deepened. 'Guess that means we'll be staying the night.'

CHAPTER NINE

STAYING the night. In Matt's house. Just her and him and…
Ellie's pulse leapt. *And…? And* if she wanted, she could let
herself go for once and give in to this attraction.

One night with Matt McGregor.

She steeled herself to hold his gaze and that now-familiar
current of energy arced across the space between them, sparking flashes of anticipation along every nerve ending. 'I'll need
to collect a few things on the way.'

His eyes twinkled with something like amusement. 'I have
a spare toothbrush.'

Her jaw firmed at the timely reminder. She just bet he did.
Probably a whole box for all those unexpected female guests
who slept over. She refused to let the doubt demons get to her.
Tonight Ellie was going to be that guest, and tonight was all
that mattered.

'And an efficient underfloor heating system,' he went on
smoothly. 'So you don't need a thing.'

No, she didn't imagine she did. She crossed her arms beneath her breasts. 'I hope the view's worth it.'

His gaze flicked briefly to the cleavage she'd unwittingly
created, then just as quickly back to her face. 'Oh, it will be,
I assure you.'

Her nipples tingled and tightened as heat spurted up her
neck, bled into her cheeks. Were they talking about the same

thing? She'd not participated in this kind of sexual innuendo in more than two years. Not since Heath…

'Grab your jacket and I'll meet you out front in a few minutes.'

She grabbed her backpack from the couch in the lounge room, her problems shoved to the back of her mind and a sense of anticipation rocketing through her as she slipped a cardigan over her sweater and dragged on her jacket before hurrying downstairs.

He'd changed and wore a black leather bomber jacket over his white T-shirt and jeans and was holding two helmets. The evening breeze slid through his spiked hair, giving it a reckless windswept edge. He looked more than a little bit dangerous.

Her heart skidded to a halt, then resumed at twice its speed. Beneath the canopy of inky sky with a whiff of motor oil in her nostrils and the throaty sound of the black-and-silver monster warming up beside him…well, it felt like some sort of illicit fantasy.

He must have transferred that recklessness to her. The spine-tingling prospect of freedom and being with Matt on that metallic beast as he whisked her away from reality… Just for tonight she wanted to forget everything and enjoy the ride—and it wasn't only the bike she was thinking of.

As he settled the helmet on her head, helped her adjust it, she admitted, 'I've never been game enough to ride on a motorbike.'

He climbed on, turned the key, patted the seat behind him. 'It's easy,' he said over the noise. 'Just hang on and let me do the rest.'

Still, perching herself behind him—

'Closer,' he ordered, voice muffled through the helmet as she wiggled into place. 'Don't be shy.'

Easy for you to say, your private parts aren't touching mine. She did as he requested, scooting close. His body heat warmed her inner thighs through the double layer of denim, her hands slid around his waist and over the soft leather.

At first the ride jerked and twisted as they crossed the suburbs, stopping for traffic lights and accelerating away at what felt like breathtaking speed but probably wasn't. But once they hit open road she relaxed, leaning into his sheltering body, revelling in the way the chill wind snuck under her visor and skimmed over her knees.

The cold was exhilarating, invigorating and a stunning contrast to his warmth all down the front of her body. The monotonous hum of the powerful machine vibrated through her bones, soothing her into a soporific state of well-being.

They stopped briefly near Geelong for hot coffee and cruised down Lorne's main street soon after midnight. A moment later Matt extended one arm to the view at the top of a crest in the road where she saw white foam curling and crashing over worn rocks along the shoreline.

A short distance from the township Matt turned off the main road and followed a track through tall skinny eucalypts, coming to a stop in front of a sprawling dwelling cleverly camouflaged to blend with its surroundings. He parked beneath a wide verandah, switched off the ignition.

Ellie climbed off, removed her helmet. Salty air heavy with the fragrance of eucalyptus swept through her hair and filled her nostrils. After the noisy journey the sudden silence rang with the sounds of the bush. An animal scuttled through the undergrowth, the soft clack of higher branches as the wind buffeted treetops, all against the background sound of distant surf. A gibbous moon spangled the leaves with silver.

'Here we are. Home sweet home.'

He produced a key and unlocked the front door, flipped a switch, illuminating dozens of downlights, giving the room a mellow ambience as she followed him in.

It had to be the most unique home she'd ever seen, all odd

angles and glass and slabs of colour that blended with the natural environment outside. A ceiling that soared and dipped, invoking a feeling of space and movement. 'No walls.'

'Don't need them.'

Her brows rose in surprise. 'Not even the bathroom?'

He grinned. 'The exception. Through here.'

Huge. With a spa big enough to need its own lifeguard, double shower, double vanity. It was another fantasy of glass, but private at the same time, and looked out onto a roomy columned courtyard of lush native flora accessed only through the bathroom.

'*Cyathea australis.*'

'If you say so.' Matt grinned. 'I prefer to call them tree ferns. It's easier to say.'

'You designed all this?' she said, following him to the living space.

He nodded, removing his jacket, tossing it over a wide leather couch. 'It's flexible in that I can add modules to extend living space as required. This suits me fine as it is for now.'

Ellie stared at the expensive fittings, the flow of honeyed wooden flooring. 'Not bad for a weekender.'

'Not a weekender,' he said. 'It's my home. I want you to see the view of the bay from upstairs.' He led her up a shallow flight of floating steps to the mezzanine level. Her feet made no sound as she crossed the thick carpet. The huge irregular hexagonal window framed a spectacular view of Louttit Bay filmed with moon glow. Lorne's lights twinkled through the trees. Possums partied on the roof, their bush sounds the only noise in the room's silence.

'Now isn't that a sight for inspiration?' He was standing close behind her, his voice rumbling softly at her ear.

'Oh, yeah.' His warmth spread across her back like a blanket. She placed a hand against the glass. So many contrasts. Heat and cold, the dark rise of the land against the moon-drenched water. Man-made in harmony with nature. And the man who'd built it all slid his hands loosely around her waist. Strength and tenderness. She didn't need protecting, but it was there in the way he shielded her with his body.

His hands now on her shoulders, he turned her to face him. 'Ellie.' Her name had never sounded as beautiful as it did coming from his lips. And the sight of this gorgeous man before her was more inspiring than any view behind.

And more terrifying.

She'd sworn never again to allow a man to seduce her and here she was. Yet staring up at him she sensed no intended seduction as such. Just a burning desire. One he'd carefully banked. One she shared.

She didn't need a man, yet in this moment, with the starlight reflecting in his eyes and the cool night radiating through the glass at her back, she wanted *this* man.

Neither did she need his support—unless it was the kind of support which would keep her upright on legs that were weakening with every beat of her pulse.

His hands slid over her shoulders, her arms, then inside her jacket, palms brushing the sides of her breasts, every fingertip sending sparks of excitement shooting to her feminine places.

What she needed… She *needed* his hands on more of her. On all of her. Her own hands trembled as they followed the hard contours of his chest through the soft jersey of his T-shirt. Up…until she felt his heart thud fast and heavy beneath her palm.

The fragrance of the cold night's ride clung to his clothes, his skin. Leaning up on tiptoe, she breathed him in, right in the little hollow at the base of his neck. Dizzy with his scent, his proximity, she dropped her head on his chest.

Her whole body throbbed with heavy anticipation, yet she felt as light as air, as if the slightest puff would blow her away.

Had she ever felt this way? She might have thought so once, but she couldn't have—she'd have remembered something this intense.

Cupping her face in both hands, he tilted it towards him, and what a view she was treated to. A strong jaw etched in the moon's silver glow, hair backlit with gold from the light filtering up from downstairs, lips that no artist could do justice to, eyes as dark as midnight. Eyes that could make a girl forget how to breathe, let alone her well-rehearsed lessons in self-preservation.

He whisked a thumb over her lips, just once. 'What do you want, Ellie?'

Be careful what you wish for. The little warning voice she'd learned to listen to and followed religiously dulled to a whisper, then faded completely.

One night. Her choice. Her decision.

Stepping out of his arms, she shrugged out of her jacket, let it fall to the floor. 'You. Here. Now.'

If it were possible, his eyes darkened further, but he didn't move except to let his arms drop to his sides. 'Are you sure? Because I don't know if I can stop if—'

'Yes, I'm sure,' she snapped out, unbuttoning her cardigan. She had no illusions about Matt where relationships were concerned, but now she'd made her decision she wanted to get on with it. 'One night.' She lifted her chin, every cell in her body jangling. 'That's the way you play the game, isn't it? One night at a time?'

He hesitated, the acknowledgement written on his face as he rocked back on his heels. 'But I'm not sure it's the way you do.'

No, it wasn't, but the other way hadn't worked for her in the past so perhaps it was time she tried something different. Knowing it all up-front meant no expectations, no disappointments and, most important of all, no broken heart. Without breaking eye contact she slipped off her cardigan. 'Wasn't it you who suggested the other day that we do something about this…tension between us? Get it out of the way?'

'Yes, but after what happened, you might—'

'I'm calling you on it now. I want to forget this afternoon.' Still watching him, she toed off her sneakers, peeled off her socks. Her toes curled into the warm carpet. 'I feel like I'm about to explode. I still have all this pent-up angry energy I need to get rid—'

Matt cut her off with a hard-mouthed kiss that echoed the wildness he sensed within her, barely glimpsing her surprised eyes as he dragged her against him and answered her request.

She didn't miss a beat, meeting him with the same force, the same heat, the same passion. Her hands shot upward, clutching fistfuls of his T-shirt, lush lips parting beneath his, tongues touching, tangling, thrusting in a tantalising prelude to what he wanted to do with her. To her. In her.

The hot potent flavour of her residual anger flowed over his tastebuds like dark chilli chocolate as he searched out all the hidden recesses in her mouth while his hands explored the firm flesh beneath her skinny T-shirt. Curves he'd not expected, dips he'd never seen, made all the more enticing by his long-endured anticipation—a neat little bellybutton, the indentation he discovered at the base of her spine when he slid a hand below the waistband of her jeans.

Breaking the kiss, he lifted his head, watched the same anticipation colour her eyes that deep dark amethyst he found so fascinating. Skimming his palms up her sides and taking her T-shirt along the way, he dragged it off, tossed it over his shoulder, leaving only her locket winking erotically above her cleavage.

A glimpse of white lace bra before he yanked it down to her waist so he could bury his face in the smooth fragrant valley between her luscious breasts, cupping their weight, then massaging them so that her nipples beaded tightly against the centre of his palms.

Her low keening moan triggered a thousand impatient needs, a thousand desperate desires. Dazed and driven by his own impatience to get naked right along with her, he dragged his T-shirt over his head. 'Jeans off, now.'

He watched her shimmy out of her jeans and a pair of cute white knickers with hearts on while he discarded his boots, then shoved down his own.

Like a man dying of starvation, his eyes devoured her body, shimmering in the room's soft glow. Shadows and light. Exquisite. Perfection.

Where have you been all my life?

The question hovered on the edge of his mind, unsettling him momentarily. He dragged his gaze back to her face, reminding himself she was here now, his to enjoy, his to pleasure. Reminding himself that he didn't measure his relationships by time, but by mutual satisfaction and respect.

So why did he hesitate to touch? Why did his hand shake when he reached out to trace a line down her body, from cheek to collarbone and over her left breast where he stopped to feel her heart thud in time with his?

Her eyes were taking their own erotic journey—he could almost feel the caress—a hot silk glove stroking his erection to almost unbearable hardness.

'Don't stop now,' she demanded.

He looked down at himself, choked out a half-laugh, then met her eyes once more. 'Do I look like I want to stop?'

'No...' Her eyes sparked with arousal.

His eyes remained on hers as he reached for her hands, drew her against him. And in that first glorious instant when her body melted against his, warm and willing and all woman, his toes curled off the carpet and he shuddered to the soles of his feet. When she gasped and plucked at his shoulders, he answered with a groan that seemed to come from the depths of his being.

Desire clashed with passion, impatience with hunger. His mouth fused with hers. Bodies bumping, legs tangling, he manoeuvred them both backwards and collapsed onto the bed, Ellie sprawled over him.

He twisted so that she lay beneath him, plundering her mouth while his hands raced over her. She writhed against him, her small deft fingers scraping over his neck, his shoulders, the base of his spine. Her warm fragrance teased his nostrils; her breathing was fast and shallow.

Impatience tore at him. He couldn't get enough. Enough of her scent, her moans, her taste. The room's cool air mingled with the warm scent of arousal, muted light spilled over them like gold dust and her skin glowed like fire.

The primitive race to finish what they'd begun beat like a jungle drum through his blood, vanquishing any semblance of his customary urbane finesse.

No time to linger, less to think. Pushing her legs apart with his thigh, he plunged his fingers into her wet heat… *Protection.*

The world they'd created ground to a halt.

On a groan of frustration, he withdrew his hand. 'Condom,' he mumbled when she whimpered in protest. He reared up, yanking open his bedside drawer and pulling out the necessary item.

Ellie bit her lip at the unavoidable delay, momentarily appalled that she'd not given it a thought. But before she could chastise herself, his hard body was stretched over hers once more, his weight pressing her into the mattress.

He drove inside her, one long swift glide that had her bucking to meet him and gasping his name. She lifted her eyes and his all-dark, all-seeing, all-powerful gaze met hers. And in that stunning singular instant of mutual connection she surrendered freely.

He withdrew, then plunged again, deeper, harder. Closer.

Wrapping her legs around his waist, she let him set a rhythm and take her where he would. From the dark erotic realms of her most secret fantasies to the giddy heights of mindless pleasure. She'd never wanted the way she wanted Matt McGregor, never needed anything or anyone the way she needed him at this moment.

He bewildered her. He captivated her.

He lifted her on wings of wonder and sent her soaring. Muttering her name like an oath, he thrust one final time before spinning over the edge and joining her.

Ellie's body still throbbed with the aftermath of great sex. Her skin still tingled; her breathing was still shallow. In the dimness, with only the moon's glow casting an oblique path across the carpet, they lay close, but not touching. Not speaking. Her mind was overflowing with jumbled thoughts.

The space Matt had put between them was subtle, but not lost on Ellie. A reminder that what they'd shared was simple lust, nothing more. A diversion. *Ride till you come to the end of the road.*

They'd reached that point. She'd prepared for that, been ready for it. She'd even initiated it. Yet somewhere along that journey she'd lost a part of herself. To him. Had he noticed? She listened to his breathing become slow and regular as he drifted towards sleep. She hoped not. Good Lord, the last thing she needed was for him to think she expected more than what they'd shared. Sex. Good sex. *Very* good sex.

That was all.

She sighed into the silence, resisting the urge to curl up against him and reconnect in a physical if not sexual way. To her, intimacy was as important as the sex. But not for Matt.

She reminded herself again that she didn't expect more. Problem was, she'd never used sex as a diversion for her problems. She didn't know the etiquette for the morning after. Or the day after. Belle was due back Monday. Then Matt would leave and that would be it. The end. *Finito*.

And if that hurt and left her feeling empty and alone, she'd have no-one to blame but herself.

Matt stared up at the low-beamed ceiling, resisting the urge to scoop Ellie closer. Already his sex stirred to life. He wanted to tuck her bottom against him and take her from behind—slowly this time, while he— *No. Deep slow breaths*. He needed to clear the confusion of thoughts and feelings from his mind before he did.

He'd thought once he'd had her, this attraction between them would settle. He'd get on with his life, she with hers. Instead, his response had been…unnerving.

Hell, this whole impulsive idea to bring her here had been a one-off. He'd never brought a woman to his place. Not for sex, not for any reason. His bush home was his private refuge. Belle was the only woman he allowed to get close.

His thoughts shifted to Angela. She'd seemed to be everything he wanted in a woman. Sophisticated, bright and intelligent. Until she'd told him she wanted more than a no-strings relationship. She'd wanted marriage, the house in the 'burbs, the kids and the dog.

She'd wanted the promise of everlasting love.

His fists tightened against the mattress but he forced himself to remain still. He'd been unable to give it to her and he'd had to let her go when she told him she wouldn't accept less.

What did Ellie want?

She turned towards him in sleep, shifting nearer. Too near. One arm slid over his chest and a breast snugged up against his torso. Intimacy and trust. His body tightened further. He closed his eyes, refusing to acknowledge it. Despite her assertion to the contrary, he had an edgy feeling Ellie wasn't the kind of woman who'd be satisfied with a fling either. He'd allowed himself to get too close on an emotional level. Dangerously close.

It was a long time before he slept.

CHAPTER TEN

THERE really was nothing quite like waking up next to a warm woman on a winter's morning. Particularly if that woman had hair that smelled of hyacinths and a firm smooth bottom snuggled against his hardening groin.

Unlike last night, the room glowed with a crimson dawn. Rather than the possum party, a couple of kookaburras exchanged a cheery good-morning in the gums outside the window.

But the urgency hadn't lessened. If anything, it had increased. Again Matt was hit with the same headlong, mind-blowing rush to have her. That same sweet desperation to bury himself inside her.

He fought the feeling down, throwing off the bedclothes, welcoming the cooler air over his heated flesh. He needed to get out of here, away from temptation. She did things to him he didn't want, didn't need. 'Time to rise and shine,' he said, forcing a brightness he didn't feel into his voice. 'Why don't you take the first shower. I'll make us some breakfast. I want to be on the road asap.'

'Okay.' Ellie half expected him to ask if he could join her, but no matter how attentive he'd been last night and how sensational their lovemaking, she'd sensed the barrier he'd put between them. She told herself it was a relief, *not* a disappointment. He played it casual, she would too. That's what they'd agreed to.

From beneath the covers, she watched him stroll naked to the mirrored wardrobe and pull out a thick aubergine dressing gown. That butt was magnificent, no doubt about it. Tight, taut. Tantalisingly touchable. She'd known that, but she'd only seen glimpses. Her imagination had filled in the gaps. Now, seeing him for the first time in all his glory in the full light of day… Then he turned around, and, oh, my…

He was an architectural masterpiece in himself. Hard planes over well-defined muscle, sharp angles that caught the early sunlight filtering through the window and cast navy shadows in dips and hollows. Not to mention all that…that glorious masculinity.

No, not to mention that at all. Swallowing, she struggled to pull her lust-crazed thoughts into some sort of order. Then he stepped into a pair of boxers and her lip-sucking moment was over.

She realised he'd picked up her discarded clothes while she'd been lying here like lady of the manor. He laid them at the foot of the bed with the robe. 'You'll find towels in the bathroom.'

'Thanks.' That wild fantasy of making him her love slave surfaced and she fought down a blush, but it wouldn't have mattered because he gave her no more than a glance.

She waited till he'd pulled on jeans before easing herself off the bed, clutching her clothes to her breasts and heading to the bathroom.

Ellie soaped herself up beneath the hot spray with exquisite care, every dab, every glide of her hands over her skin, a reminder of another pair of hands. Her body quite literally sang.

A tiny flash of movement caught her eye through the

fogged glass. She cleared a space and saw a black-and-yellow honeyeater flitting in and out of the courtyard's fernery.

She could get used to this, she thought. Shaking her head she switched off the taps with unnecessary force and reached for a towel. Forget it. Wasn't going to happen. Wouldn't know what to do with it if it did.

Because it would end. It always ended.

She tugged at the tangled curls, secured her hair at the back of her head with an elastic this morning and stared at her own face in the mirror. 'Repeat after me,' she told her reflection. *'Don't be fooled again, Ellie Rose. Guys like Matt aren't looking for long-term with girls like you.'*

Matt had breakfast in the oven and ready to dish up when his mobile rang. 'Hello.'

'Matthew.'

He smiled at the sound of the familiar voice. ''Lo, Belle. How's everything going?'

'Very well, dear. Or it was, but there's a bit of a problem here.'

'What's wrong?' His hand hovered over the stove, breakfast forgotten. 'Anything I can do?'

'No, no. It's just that Miriam wanted to go skydiving and she talked me into—'

'You did *what*?'

'You heard correctly,' she said with a smile in her voice. 'If ninety-year-olds can do it, why not me? When you get to my age you realise that sometimes you have to take chances before it's too late. It was a tandem dive with a fully qualified instructor. Anyway,' she hurried on before Matt could get another word in, 'Miriam landed heavily and twisted her ankle. She lives alone and I'd like to stay on a day or two to help but I don't want to put you out longer than I have to.'

'No need to hurry back. Everything's fine here.'

'That's good to hear.' She paused. 'How's Eloise?'

He smiled at her usual formality. 'Fine. The weather's been a bit wet for gardening but I kept her busy.' He was suddenly excruciatingly aware of how his response might be interpreted, so he added, 'Your windows now sparkle.'

'Oh. Thank her for me.' Pause. 'Matthew…I know when you're not saying something… Have you been seeing her?'

Seeing her— Oh, yeah, images of last night were imprinted on his eyeballs. 'She works for you, Belle, of course I have.'

'You know what I mean.'

'Don't go getting any romantic ideas, Belle.' He struggled with a feeling that he was scaling his own skyscraper with one hand tied behind his back. 'It's not…'

Then he noticed Ellie in the doorway, looking unsure, and Belle's voice faded into the background. He beckoned her in. How long had she been standing there? What had she heard? And while he tried to recall what he'd said, he watched the way her nipples poked at her T-shirt as she stretched and studied the view from the window and everything else flew out of his mind.

He turned away, rattled off, 'Have to go, Belle. We're about to have breakfast. Talk to you soon, bye.'

Ellie's arms dropped and she spun to him, the pleasure bleaching from her face. 'Oh, that's just peachy. Breakfast? You as good as told Belle, my *employer*, we're sleeping together. Slept together,' she corrected quickly, her eyes widening as if remembering that was all they'd agreed to.

'I didn't mention any names.' His voice felt tight as he dropped the phone onto the table. 'And so what if we did? We're consenting adults.' While Ellie sat down, he concentrated on sliding a plate piled with crisp bacon, eggs and buttered toast from the oven. He set it in front of her. 'Eat before it gets cold.'

She bit into a piece of toast. 'What about you?'

He moved away from her fresh scent before he said or did something unwise. 'I'm going to take a shower first.' With the safety of distance, he grinned, but it felt forced. 'Leave some bacon for me.'

They'd ridden back to Melbourne soon after breakfast, arriving at Belle's midmorning. Now Matt scowled at the garden in progress through the window while he spoke to a guy he knew about finding Ellie new accommodation.

He'd dropped Ellie back at her apartment. The cleaning crew had been; Matt had ensured her door was repaired and secure. Then he'd left. No suggestion of meeting up later. Nothing.

With arrangements to view a couple of places, he disconnected. He'd give her a call later, make sure everything was okay. Meanwhile there was a problem at one of the Sydney sites that couldn't wait. He'd already made arrangements to fly there. Business was his priority, always had been—he'd see Ellie Tuesday.

Days away. He frowned. Memories of last night played over and over in his mind. How smooth and soft her skin felt against his when she'd wrapped her legs around him. Her impatient moans of passion against his ear. Her slick hot heat as he'd plunged inside her. She'd been so responsive, so satisfying. The best sex ever. From her response she thought so too.

Why wait for Tuesday?

Swiping up his keys, he headed out into the drab winter's day.

'Matt.' Ellie pulled her door wider, staring at the man who'd left less than an hour ago. 'Did you forget something?'

'As a matter of fact...' He stepped in, closing the door

behind him and pulled her close, crushing her breasts against his chest and covering her mouth with his.

If she'd thought he'd changed his mind after last night, this hot, hard doubt-melting kiss proved her wrong. He lifted his head. 'It doesn't have to be one night, Ellie,' he murmured, cruising his hands up her back.

'What are you saying?' As if she didn't know.

As if she could think of the right response...the *sensible* response. After all, she'd heard him telling Belle not to get any romantic ideas...and despite their mutual understanding—that last night was one night and one night only—it had hurt. More than it should.

'We could spend a few more days...and nights...enjoying getting to know each other better.'

She felt the demand in his fingers and stared up into impatient dark eyes. Less than twelve hours ago she'd seen passion burning bright in those eyes. It was still there, dark and smouldering. One move, one spark, and they'd ignite.

She wanted to burn like that with him again.

But a few days, then what? He was talking about a few hours of pleasure between the sheets with maybe the odd candlelit dinner thrown in. And when put like that...was she *really* considering turning him down?

But something inside her cramped and twisted and she stepped back. Did she want to relive that familiar pain of being left behind when he moved on? To slice open those old wounds around her heart which had never completely healed?

He was suggesting a fling.

She didn't do flings. And she didn't do them for very good reasons.

She continued to back away until her backside hit the edge of the kitchen table. 'I know what you're asking.' *And you want to put a time limit on it.* 'Forget it. I enjoyed last night, and I would be lying to pretend otherwise, but—'

His mouth swooped down on hers again, cutting off her protests. His beautiful, beguiling, bewitching mouth. Tormenting her with all kinds of sweet temptation, promising all manner of dreamy delights. Delights he'd barely begun to show her last night, delights she'd barely begun to discover.

She wanted more. And he gave her more, with mouth and tongue, low-throated murmurs and clever hands. Not the blazing brush fire this time, but a hot steady burn, no less powerful in its intensity.

When he lifted his head and looked straight and clear into her eyes, she found herself clinging to his sweatshirt for support. Her head was spinning, her heart trying to catch up.

'It was good between us last night,' he murmured. 'I want to pursue it. So do you.'

She closed her eyes, denying it, denying him. Denying herself. 'No.'

'Look me dead in the eye and tell me you don't want to continue what we started.'

He cupped her jaw, thumbs whisking over her lips, and her brain shut down. 'I don't want you to—' one hand skimmed down the centre of her body from neck to navel, down '—to… stop,' she finished on a moan. She tried to move away again, but the table prevented her and it seemed her body had a will of its own. 'I can't think when you do that.…'

'Then look at me, be honest and tell me you don't want me.' The trace of his lips over her chin and down the side of her neck had her arching backwards over the table, his hand warm against her lower belly. Her feminine places swelled and throbbed. One touch and she was melting.…

Her eyes drifted open. 'This is crazy.'

'I agree.'

He lifted his head, watched her with a grin that promised everything she wanted if only she had the courage to take it for however long it lasted.

He wiggled his brows. 'Why don't we get crazy to-gether?'

She felt her own lips kick up at the corners. 'You think it'd help? I mean…help with getting it out of our systems. Like you said.' Sometime. She waved a vague hand; she couldn't remember when he'd said it, only that he had. Which meant he wanted to get naked with her to scratch that pesky clichéd itch. Temporary diversion. Lust.

'We could give it another try right now…' He shifted closer, easing himself between her thighs.

'Uh-uh. Not until we make a few things clear.' Pushing him away, she straightened, her mind awhirl. Did she dare to risk setting herself up for the fall which would inevitably occur? For starters, 'If I change my mind, you respect that, no questions asked.'

He nodded. 'You got it.'

'And while we're being crazy together, you're not being crazy with anyone else.'

'Ellie, I—'

She shook her head. 'Never. *Ever.* I won't tolerate it.' She could feel herself shaking, her voice catching, remembering Heath's betrayal. While he'd made merry with her, he'd had a fiancée he'd forgotten to tell her about. 'I'll not—'

'Ellie, calm down. I'm not asking for undying love and commitment. All I'm asking is a few days of mutual enjoy-ment. Just you and me.'

'A few days.' She stared up at him, unable to believe he'd ask it, unable to believe she'd even consider it, let alone agree to it.

'It'll be okay, Ellie.' He searched her gaze for the longest time, then touched her cheek with a light finger. It was almost as if he knew she'd been hurt before, and his perception and understanding did strange things to her insides, quieting the shrill questions and fears, beckoning to her like a warm quilt on a cold night.

Still, she rubbed the tiny shiver from her arms that his touch invoked. 'I know it will.' She'd make sure of it.

He nodded, taking her reply as acceptance. 'I need to return to Sydney for work for a couple of days. Come with me.'

She felt her jaw drop. 'To Sydney? What about Belle?'

He smiled. 'I happen to know she'd approve.'

'I don't know that she would—what about her kitchen garden? Thanks to the weather, it's behind schedule. She's trusting me to get on with the job in her absence.'

'You're not due to work again until next week. I've organised the company jet to be ready at three-thirty and booked a table for dinner tonight at the Sydney Tower Restaurant.'

Company jet. Dinner in Sydney.

And his undivided attention.

An incredulous laugh bubbled up. She was standing here in her dim, decrepit one-room apartment, being propositioned by an irresistible millionaire who'd already planned the entire thing. It was all moving so fast she felt as if she was being whisked up to the top of that tower already. 'Mr Super Confident,' she murmured.

'The only way to make things happen.'

How was she going to keep up with him? 'I don't have anything suitable to wear to such an up-market restaurant, and didn't you say you had to work?'

'Not till tomorrow. And you'll look gorgeous, whatever you wear.'

Oh, yeah? He hadn't seen her wardrobe. 'You work on a Sunday?'

'It's urgent and the only day everyone involved can fit it in. You can sightsee, shop or spend the time at the apartment, if you prefer. There's a spa with a great view over the city and plenty of bubbles.'

'Soap or champagne?'

'Both, if you so desire.'

And, oh, she did… She bit back a sigh. Her own *Pretty Woman* vision without the shopping spree.

Unlike the crowds and delays of commercial travel, they departed on time and with no fuss, leaving the dull grey Melbourne skyline behind.

Soon after take-off Matt fixed them drinks and nibbles, then excused himself to catch up on some work on his laptop, leaving Ellie to lie back on the wide leather seat and enjoy the comfort of the tiny private jet.

She watched the ice-cream clouds below them for a time, then flicked through a couple of architectural magazines. McGregor Architectural Designs featured on the cover of the previous month's issue. Matt was standing at the base of some steps, jacket slung over his shoulder, a glimmer of that sexy-as-all-get-out grin on his face. A needle-thin glass-and-steel pyramid vaulted into the sky behind him. She recognised it as one of the city's prominent buildings, but hadn't realised it was one of Matt's designs and the home of his business empire. The whole concept that she was in his jet, flying off to spend the weekend with him, blew her away.

In just over an hour they were descending over the Harbour Bridge, the water reflecting the deepening orange and indigo sky. Lights were coming on all over the city like thousands of twinkling fireflies.

A limousine picked them up and whisked them to the city centre. They stopped in front of a tall round building and stepped out onto George Street, thronged with tourists out on a Saturday night. The lobby sparkled with lights and black granite. Ellie had worked in Sydney but she'd stayed in cheap accommodation, not in…this. 'You own an apartment in this building too?' she asked as they stepped into the elevator.

'Yes.'

'How many places does one guy need?'

He grinned as they shot skyward. 'I look at them as investments and it beats impersonal and unfamiliar hotel rooms.'

The elevator doors slid open to reveal a small lobby. Matt opened a wide-panelled door and the stunning harbour view greeted them through floor-to-ceiling windows. As she followed him through the spacious apartment she noticed vibrant autumn colours of amber and taupe. A tall arrangement of black lacquered twigs in a vermilion pot stood in one corner. Comfortable couches, the latest in electronic entertainment.

He stopped at a bedroom, setting their bags just inside the door. Her pulse stepped up at the sight of the king-size bed with its dark-chocolate quilt and apricot pillows.

The reason she was here.

The air crackled with sexual awareness but he said, 'Feel free to make yourself at home. I've got some plans to go over before tomorrow morning. I'll be in my study.' *Business before pleasure.*

'Okay.' She closed her eyes briefly as he left, feeling way out of her comfort zone. *What was she doing?* She wasn't the type of girl who went with a rich man for sex.

She crossed the room to watch the changing colours of the twilight sky. Last night Matt had been just a regular guy in a leather jacket who rode bikes to relax. The guy who'd slipped over in the mud with her. The guy who'd helped her wipe the mess off her kitchen floor when she'd been burgled and looked after her when she was ill.

Here on his own turf, this Matt was someone else. The permanent playboy and businessman, wealthier than she'd ever imagined, more influential than she'd given him credit for. He managed a business empire over two cities. A man way out of her stratosphere.

He was also the man she'd had the steamiest, most sensational sex of her life with.

If she could just concentrate on that and *not* think about how he was tugging at strings she didn't want tugged. Making her feel things she didn't want to feel. Making her vulnerable.

No, no, no. Not vulnerable. In control. Swinging her case onto the bed, she unzipped it with a firm tug and pulled out her one and only black dress. She slid the mirrored wardrobe door open to search for a coat hanger...

A row of after five dresses met her eyes, neatly arranged in colour from black through to white. Her stomach clenched, her fingers went limp. But only for a moment. Had the woman left her designer underwear too? Throwing her own cheap cotton dress on the bed, she flung open cupboard doors, yanked out drawers, rifling through briefs, boxers, socks.

She found an abundant supply of condoms in the top bedside drawer. An overabundance, in her opinion. She slammed the drawer shut. At least he was responsible, but did he have to be such a boy scout about it?

'Ellie? I heard noises. What are you doing?'

She swivelled her head to see Matt the love rat at the doorway. The way he stared at her, brow furrowed, eyes questioning... Damn it, he made her feel as if she was looking for his hidden stash of cash.

She realised she was holding a pair of black briefs and dropped them back in the drawer. Lifted her hands away from his underwear.

'The condoms are in the top drawer,' he said, leaning lazily against the doorjamb. 'In case you were wondering.'

'Yes, I *know*. I was *wondering* why you've asked me here when you've clearly got plenty of female company to keep you occupied.'

His gaze followed hers to the open wardrobe and his expression cleared. 'I forgot to mention them. They're for you to choose something to wear this evening. I had the boutique from downstairs bring them up, but if the size isn't right…' He trailed off at her glare.

'So my clothes aren't good enough?' She felt like three kinds of an idiot, accusing him without cause.

He frowned. 'You were the one who said you didn't have anything suitable to wear.'

Oh. Right. 'I didn't expect… Look…I'm sorry, okay?' She waved a vague hand at the jumbled drawers. 'I don't need you to—'

'Just choose something. That purple or the turquoise.' His voice rumbled, water-smoothed stones beneath a deep-flowing river.

She could almost hear him say, *One that comes off easily at the end of the evening.* Could see it in the way his eyes seared her skin.

Or maybe he was saying, *We can be late.…*

All the air left her lungs. She was tempted, so tempted, to walk on over and push his T-shirt up, kiss her way across that firm, hard abdomen and distract him from his work.… 'Okay,' she heard herself murmur as if she stood somewhere outside of herself.

He gave her a heated look, but then, just when she thought she'd been right all along, he glanced at his watch. 'We'll leave in thirty minutes.'

CHAPTER ELEVEN

POISED three hundred metres above Sydney, the scenery from the tower's restaurant was, as always, spectacular. Matt barely glanced at it, preferring to watch the city lights reflected in Ellie's eyes. To linger over the way her lips curved when she talked and admire the play of light and shadow over her cleavage in that low-cut turquoise dress.

She was different from other women he'd dated. What she lacked in sophistication she made up for in her enthusiasm. She had an appetite for the sumptuous food on offer, unlike most who picked over the salads and talked about the latest diet fad. Ellie talked about her hopes to set up a landscaping business, a financial struggle the power women in his life would never have to cope with.

She had an in-depth knowledge of environmental issues, natural and herbal remedies and sixties music. She loved her volunteer work with the kids. She loved sci-fi movies but preferred reading fantasy novels and could name every character in *Lord of the Rings* without missing a beat.

She just kept surprising him.

He let his mega-dollar-a-bottle champagne swirl over his tongue and wondered how many more surprises she had in store while he watched her break her last prawn apart with as much care as he'd seen her tend her coriander seedlings. She popped the seafood in her mouth, then dipped her fingers in the water bowl supplied, wiped each one individually on her napkin. Those small slender fingers fascinated him. He shifted on his chair, remembering the feel of them on his body last night.

And they'd barely scratched the surface, so to speak. His skin heated, his neck prickled, his groin hardened. So much to discover, so little time…

Her eyes lifted to his, warm and liquid and almost black in the light, and he knew without a shadow of doubt that their thoughts were speeding in the same direction.

She continued to watch him with those expressive eyes while she patted her mouth with her napkin. 'That was wonderful.'

'The evening's barely begun.' He dropped his own napkin on the table. 'You ready to leave?'

A spark danced across her gaze and her full lips tilted at the edges. 'I thought you'd never ask.'

'We didn't have dessert.' Ellie's voice was breathless and hot against his ear as he backed her up against the door to his apartment before the elevator doors had closed behind them.

'Dessert's overrated.' His fingers fumbled the key while he kissed his way down the exposed column of her neck. 'I have all the sweet temptation I need right in front of me.' Then the door swung open and they stumbled inside.

He kicked it shut and, grasping her wrists, rolled her with him against the wall. Right here, right now, he gave in to the firestorm which had been raging through him all evening. Beneath his skin and in his blood.

He pinned her hands above her head so he could feel all of her, from mouth to breasts to thighs and knees. Then he leaned in, grinding his erection against her softness and crushing her mouth with his until they were both delirious and dizzy and drunk on desire.

She tasted of hot wine and hotter woman and something darker, richer, more potent. One hand traced the sinuous length of an arm, from fingertip to palm, elbow to shoulder, pausing where her pulse beat a crazy tattoo at her neck, then down over one breast, to enjoy its firm fullness, loving the way she arched urgently against his palm. He tugged her closer.

All of her. He wanted all of her. Again. And in that moment of stunning contact he forgot caution, forgot that he always maintained a certain emotional distance. He wanted to give her all. Everything. Until they were both spent and neither had anything left to give. 'What you do to me,' he managed, between laboured breaths, 'should be against the law.'

'So arrest me.' Her husky voice laced with humour stirred the simmering volcano in his gut to a rolling boil.

His laugh was strained. He drew back a moment to take in the vision before him. With her arms still above her head and against the wall of their own accord, she looked like a siren calling him home. In the light slanting through the windows from the city below, he could see the sheen of desire on her face and arms. Her eyes were open and dazed and full of passion.

His fingers tensed, then twisted into the soft fabric at her waist. Curves and contours, dips and valleys—he found them all. A mess of contradictions, he wanted his hands everywhere at once, yet he wanted to savour each sensation to its fullest.

No time.

Reaching out, she grabbed a handful of his shirt. Buttons popped, he heard a rip, then her hands rushed up and over his chest.

She made a sound—part humour, part apology. 'I hope that wasn't your best shirt.'

'I have more.' Sweeping her up into his arms, he staggered

to the bedroom, his shirt hanging from his arms. Her fast shallow breaths fuelled his own. Impatience, as urgent as if it were the first time, whipped through him.

She reached around to her back, the action thrusting her breasts forward. He heard the rasp of a zipper. His hands slipped beneath the straps and her dress slid off, a whisper of silk on skin beneath his hands. A crackle of electric excitement as the rest of their clothes were stripped away and they tumbled onto the bed together.

No words. Just mindless pleasure, mutual delight. He feasted on her dewy skin, drank the honeyed pleasure at her mouth, then on a groan that seemed to come from some uncharted place inside plunged his aching erection into her warm and willing heat.

She arched to meet him as if she'd been waiting a lifetime, clutching at his shoulders, fingernails scraping down his spine. Reaching down between their joined bodies, he touched her sweet spot and watched her eyes turn indigo. 'Matt…' Her breath sobbed out. 'I can't…'

Catching her plea on his tongue, he touched her again, tracing tiny circles over her slick moisture with his thumb. 'You can. Now.' True to his promise, seconds later her body convulsed beneath him, her gasps harsh against his neck as he sent her soaring.

'Again.' He raced with her along a dark velvet road which spun up into a never-ending spiral where the air was hot and heavy, filled with the sound of their moans.

They took what they wanted, what they needed, each from the other, flesh straining against flesh, mouths fused, hearts pounding in sync. And then the hot and slippery slide to climax.

Sated and spent, they lay close, touching. Intimate. Explosions of pleasure still shuddered through Ellie's body. So Matt wasn't into pillow talk, but he'd let down some of the barriers she'd sensed last night. Like right now as he pulled her close, his hard masculine torso warming her all down her back.

She snuggled against him, not analysing, not anticipating tomorrow or the next day, but content to simply be as sleep closed in around them.

Since Matt had left for his appointments early, Ellie spent a lazy day pleasing herself and playing tourist. Darling Harbour was within easy walking distance so she crossed Pyrmont Bridge, wandered the arcades and sat in the warm winter sun and ate ice-cream. Then she returned to the apartment and spent a couple of hours catching up on sleep in the luxurious bed they'd made love in last night and into the early morning.

Late in the afternoon she couldn't resist the lure of the spa bath. White marble surrounds, a view over the sparkling aquamarine harbour and coathanger bridge, a range of bathroom products that spoke of Matt's many hours of indulgence in this room, with or without company.

'Need your back washed?'

She turned to see Matt with a bowl of strawberries in one hand, a bottle of bubbly and two glasses in the other. He set them down and started unbuttoning his shirt. He looked gloriously masculine, his jaw shadowed with the day's stubble, his chest hair gleaming darkly in the reddening glow from the sun. His eyes smouldered with intent and her pulse leapt in anticipation. 'Only my back...?'

He undid his belt, unzipped his trousers, his erection straining against navy-blue boxers, and grinned, teeth gleaming as he pulled a condom from his pocket and held it aloft. 'Whatever you want, I'm a slave to your desires.'

Her love slave. She couldn't help the smile as she sank

back against the cool side of the bath and watched him strip away the final barriers. 'In that case...'

Afterwards, she reclined against his body while he fed her strawberries. The water lapped at her breasts. 'This is true decadence.'

He dropped a handful of bubbles onto her shoulder, smoothed it all the way down her arm. 'Enjoy it—we're leaving tomorrow morning.'

She couldn't deny the stab of disappointment. 'You finished everything here, then?'

'Yes.' Water sloshed and she felt him move as he set his glass on the tiles with a *chink*. She thought he hesitated before saying, 'Ellie, I've got a function tomorrow night at the Melbourne office. A winter solstice party. Fancy dress. Come with me.'

Her pulse skipped a happy beat, but only one. A private fling with him was one thing, being seen together in the very public arena of his place of work and amongst his colleagues was something else. That he'd asked her was another surprise and one that had her heartbeat stepping up a notch. What did it mean for her? For them?

No. She couldn't even begin thinking of them as a couple; he'd made it quite clear that's not what they were. If he was asking her to accompany him, it was because they were having a fling and he needed a partner for the evening.

But her heart squeezed tight beneath her breast. Oh, how easy it would be to step into those glass slippers and play the princess, just once. But the magic wouldn't last and no prince was going to come searching for her in the cold light of morning, least of all someone like Matt. Apart from great sex the man might as well be from another planet for all they had in common.

'Ellie?' His scratchy jaw rasped against her neck; his hands slipped beneath her armpits to play with her nipples. 'You're thinking too hard. Don't analyse it, just say yes.'

'Thanks, but I don't think so.'

His fingers stilled. Obviously he wasn't accustomed to being turned down. 'It's a charity fundraiser,' he continued. 'Right up your alley. Yasmine will be there. She's loads of fun and I know you'll like her. She's organising my costume. I'll get her to organise something and contact you.'

'Thanks, but no.' Ellie the gardener didn't want to talk to the tall, stunning Yasmine with the long sleek hair and high-profile job. 'I'm not into office parties. I'd just feel out of place.'

'Out of place? Why? Other people are bringing their partners.'

'Come on, Matt, you know what I'm talking about. We're not "partners". You and me—we're just two people having sex.'

'We're—'

'*And* we both know we're on different sides of Belle's upscale wrought-iron-and-concrete fence.'

He was silent for a long time. Then he said, 'You think that makes a difference to me?' She could feel his frown at the back of her head.

'Maybe not, but it makes a difference to me.' She shrugged, not allowing herself to look at the luxury surrounding her, not letting Matt's words seep into her consciousness and—worse, much worse—into her heart.

'Only because you let it. Who skewed your thinking, Ellie?'

'A guy I knew once.' She hadn't realised she'd spoken aloud until she felt his lips touch the back of her neck. 'And he didn't skew my thinking. He opened my eyes to the hard, real world.'

'A lover?'

'Heath.' She avoided the label. 'His name was Heath.'

'Where did you meet him?'

'I was working in a nursery-cum-florist-shop in Adelaide. He was from a wealthy family, on a working holiday from the UK, and came in to place an overseas order. We got talking. Next morning the biggest bunch of roses appeared on the counter with my name on it.

'He treated me like a princess, promised me the world all wrapped up and tied with a big red bow. Weeks later he moved in with me, even though I knew he thought my apartment was the pits, but hey, I was paying the rent, so why not?'

'He was a scumbag.'

'I thought so too.' *After he'd ripped out my heart and left me behind.* 'Especially when I learned he already had a fiancée back home—they were getting married in London the following month. I should have guessed when he placed that first order but I trusted him and it was so nice having someone in my life again.' To love and be loved. 'But it turned out I was the holiday fling. I saw everything clearly after that. I am who I am, I know my place in the world and I'm comfortable with it.'

'But not with me, apparently. Ellie, look at me.' Gripping her shoulders, he turned her to face him, tucking her legs around his muscled torso. 'Do you see a guy like Heath when you look at me?'

She looked into his eyes and answered honestly, 'No.' Unlike Heath, this man had integrity. He was honest and up-front about what he wanted.

She continued watching as the last light of the day gilded his face with bronze. And, oh, that was a big mistake—huge— because suddenly her heart that she'd closed to him was thumping in a strange and different way, ribbons of warmth spiralling around it, pulling tight. Love...

No, not that four-letter word that had no place in her life.

Ever again. Deliberately she shifted closer so that his erection nudged at the apex of her spread thighs. With her fingers she smoothed the perplexed frown from his brow, determined to hold strictly to the reason she was here with him in his bath in his luxury apartment. Determined not to think about what-ifs and ever-afters. Changing the topic. 'Enjoying sex…that's what we're good at, right?' She leaned forward and watched his eyes heat, soothed her lips against his and murmured, 'Got another of those condoms handy…?'

After Matt's chauffeured vehicle dropped her home on Monday morning, Ellie decided to take the rest of her free day to inspect a couple of job prospects advertised at the local council in today's newspaper in case the Healesville one she was looking at tomorrow didn't pan out.

Sitting around her apartment feeling sorry for herself would give her too much time to think, and she didn't want to think. She didn't have anything suitable to wear to a big-deal office party, and even if she did, she didn't fit in with those high-flying career types.

She showered and dressed in black trousers and business jacket, her mind going around in circles. Matt had been pre-occupied with work during the flight. No mention of when he'd see her again. She wondered if he'd decided to call it quits since she'd refused his party invitation. Except that now she'd have to face him when she turned up at Belle's for work.

When her mobile rang, she stood a moment, chewing on her lips. If he was trying to change her mind… But when she picked it up she didn't recognise the caller ID. 'Hello?'

'Ellie? Hi, my name's Yasmine and I work with Matt at McGregor Architectural.'

Ellie gulped, sinking onto the nearest chair, her knees turning to jelly. 'Um, hi…'

'Matt's busy right now but he asked me to give you a call

and see if I couldn't change your mind about joining our festivities this evening, and before you say no, I'll tell you now that I'm afraid if I'm unsuccessful, I could be looking for a position elsewhere tomorrow morning.'

'Oh. I—'

'Are you at home now?'

'Yes, but—'

'Great, I'm right outside on the footpath. With cake.'

'Uh…' Phone in hand, Ellie yanked her door open, hurried to the window overlooking the street at the end of the building's corridor.

And directly below her stood Yasmine, her beautiful business-clad butt on the bonnet of a sexy little silver hatchback, a phone pressed against her glorious sweep of black hair.

Ellie's fingers tightened on the phone. 'Oh, crap.'

Yasmine grinned at that, then lifted her face so that the sun worshipped her stunning cheekbones and waved up at her.

This time Ellie covered the mouthpiece, swore again, then waved back. 'Come on up.' What else could she say?

Ellie rushed back inside, decided it wasn't worth trying to make the place look presentable and, breathless, met Yasmine at the door thirty seconds later. 'Hi. Come in.'

Yasmine didn't bat an eye at her lowly apartment. 'I've been looking forward to meeting you ever since I saw you two together at the club.' She set the box from a local bakery on the table, her ring finger glittering with a starburst of diamonds.

Ellie tried not to notice the sparkly jewellery and feel pleased while she busied herself clearing the clutter of mismatched dishes to one end. 'We weren't together… I mean we were just— Matt's *talked* about me?'

'*Mentioned* you. But you know men—they never *talk*, particularly about women to other women. If only they knew it's what they *don't* say that gives them away every time.' She opened the box, revealing a selection of pastries and iced cupcakes. 'How was Sydney?'

When Ellie jerked around to stare at her, Yasmine was smiling. Grinning, actually. Showing perfect white teeth. 'Um… Great.' Snapping her mouth shut, Ellie swivelled towards the sink. 'Coffee?'

'Love one.'

Yasmine pulled out a chair and made herself at home while Ellie switched on the kettle and struggled to remember where she'd put the blasted stuff. 'How did you know? About Sydney?'

'I heard him making dinner reservations for two—best table, best wine, la-di-dah-di-dah. When he asked me to contact you this morning, I realised you're the mystery woman who's had him distracted for the past week.'

Distracted? Matt? Fingers trembling slightly, Ellie splashed hot water onto the coffee grounds, carried the mugs to the table, grabbed the spare carton of milk from the cupboard and sat down gratefully. 'But we're ju—'

'So as the event organiser, I really need you to come tonight or he's going to be absolute hell to work with tomorrow.' Yasmine slid the cakes Ellie's way. 'Help yourself to a bribe. Either that or I'll be polishing up my résumé.'

Ellie shook her head. 'I don't have anything to wear.'

'Not a problem. I have a stack of costumes in the car. There's sure to be one that fits.' She sipped her coffee, eyed Ellie over the rim of her mug. 'So, I'll just shoot downstairs and grab them, shall I? Then I have to get back to work and tell the boss the good news. At least then we might be able to put in a few productive hours before this evening.'

'I—'

'Great.' Beaming, she rose, headed for the door. 'Back in a jiff.'

Ellie blew out a slow, not-so-steady breath. It seemed Cinderella was going to the ball after all.

CHAPTER TWELVE

MATT was out of the chauffeured car the moment it pulled up outside Ellie's apartment. He tugged at the sweeping emerald cloak's tie which was all but strangling him. His hands felt a little clammy, his pulse a tad faster than usual, and for a moment he felt as if he was on his first date. And, in a way, escorting Ellie to a function as his partner for the evening *was* a first date for the two of them.

Thanks to Yasmine, colleague extraordinaire and miracle worker.

He knocked on her door. Odd—his breathing was slightly elevated while he waited for her to answer. As if he was nervous. Then the door opened and his lungs all but collapsed at the sight before him.

A petite vision in a medieval long-sleeved gown of dark crimson velvet which flowed to dainty slippered feet. A matching hooded cloak lined and trimmed with snowy fur. An ivy wreath crowned her head, tiny red berries sprinkled amongst the soft blonde hair—which was sleek and straight this evening.

He took another moment to linger in the depths of those violet eyes, sparkling with nerves tonight. Her fingers gripped the strings of the velvet pouch bag she held so tightly her knuckles were white.

'Aren't you going to say something?'

'Good evening, Ellie.' He had his breath back. Barely. And her familiar spiced-berry scent washed over him like a dream. 'You look absolutely amazing.' He kissed her cheek, respectable and civilised, the way a gentleman greets his partner on a first date. But inside…inside an unfamiliar sensation stumbled around the region of his heart. Suddenly the thought that he'd be back in Sydney in a couple of days wasn't something he wanted to think about. Tonight might be the last chance they'd have to be together.

'Thank you,' she said, bringing him back to the present. 'You're looking pretty sensational yourself.'

Her gaze stroked down his cloak, lingered a moment on the black-clad torso beneath. Little darts of heat prickled his skin, fed into his bloodstream, tightened his groin. *Later,* he promised silently. Later he was going to enjoy more than just her gaze.…

'The Holly King,' she said, lifting her eyes to his. 'As befitting the boss, I guess. Yasmine told me all about it. Question, though—where's the holly wreath that's supposed to be on your head?'

Grinning, he shook his head. 'I'm not a masochist.'

'Pity.' She smiled. 'I hadn't realised there was so much tradition attached to the evening. Guess it's more a northern hemisphere event.' She closed and locked the door behind her with the new deadlock he'd had fitted.

'So you and Yaz got along well, I take it?' Matt took her elbow as they descended the shabby stairwell.

'She's a good friend to you—you're lucky to have her.' Her pensive tone reminded Matt of Ellie's wandering and no doubt lonely lifestyle.

'She can be your friend too, you know.'

'I don't think that'll happen. You're leaving soon.…'

Whether it was the chill in the air or her words, he didn't

know, but something like a shiver ran down his spine as they stepped into the cold winter street.

'In you get,' he said, making an effort to lighten up as the chauffeur opened the door.

Ellie settled the cloak about her while Matt climbed in beside her. He poured a couple of glasses of champagne, handed her one. 'To a pleasant evening.'

She clinked her glass to his. 'A pleasant evening.'

Chauffeured limos, champagne en route. She marvelled at how quickly she'd become accustomed to this kind of luxury. How easily it could be taken for granted if you'd never known anything else.

She reminded herself this was a one-off as they cruised down the street and headed towards the city centre. Their destination speared into the sky, all twinkling lights and power and wealth.

'Something to wear tonight,' Matt said, drawing a rectangular velvet box from his pocket.

'Um.' Her heart stammered at the unexpected gesture. 'It's not necessary....'

'Maybe not, but I wanted to.' Relieving her of her glass, he pressed the box into her hands. 'Open it,' he told her when she didn't make a move to do so.

Her fingers felt awkward as she lifted the lid. A delicate single strand of what could only be diamonds winked at her on their bed of black satin. A bracelet that must have cost The Earth.

Stunning. Sensational. But also shockingly, outrageously expensive. How could anyone justify spending so much on a piece of jewellery? She'd live her life worrying if someone was going to steal it. Still, her fingers drifted over the stones. 'It's beautiful,' she breathed. 'But I'd never have an occasion to wear it....'

'You have tonight.' He lifted it, draped it over her wrist and fastened the clasp.

She lifted and rotated her arm, watched it glitter in the night lights. 'I wonder how many Third World children we could feed with the money it would fetch?'

'Ellie, it's not always about the money. It's a gift because I wanted to show you how much you…'

When he trailed off, she looked up at him. His expression was unreadable. Still a thrill of illicit pleasure lanced through her.

'…how much I've enjoyed having you with me this past week,' he finished. 'Please accept it for what it is.'

If she didn't know better she'd have said his voice sounded strained. Vulnerable? Nah, not Matt McGregor. Unlike her, he probably hadn't given its value a second thought.

Rather than look at him and read into his gaze something that wasn't there, she admired the bracelet's sparkle again. Looking at him would only remind her that their time together was nearly up. 'I'm sorry, I didn't mean to sound ungrateful or mercenary.' Its beauty would always be a cherished memory of this interlude in her life.

'You didn't. Not quite.' Smiling, he leaned across the seat, tilting her face so that he could plant warm lips on hers.

Interlude. Was that really all this was? she wondered as she let herself sink into the kiss. This heart-stopping, all-enveloping, all-consuming… *Careful, Ellie*. Digging her fingernails into her palms as he drew back, she turned to watch Southbank's lights reflect on the River Yarra. Yes, interlude. She wouldn't let it be anything else.

McGregor Architectural's meeting rooms on the forty-second floor, with a one-hundred-and-eighty-degree view over the city, were decked out in abundant winter greenery—rosemary, laurel, ivy, pine boughs. The forest fragrance mingled with the scent of melting wax, beer and hot cider.

Matt felt a warm feeling of satisfaction when Ellie's first impression when they stepped out of the elevator was, 'Wow.'

He'd devoted the past fifteen years to growing the business. Day and night, often seven days a week for months at a time. 'Yasmine and the organising committee have done a terrific job.' He stood a moment, enjoying the celebrations taking place in front of them, enjoying the feel of Ellie's hand in his.

Warm colours of red and amber and gold in the tall freestanding candles, rainbow hues in the sun catchers suspended from the ceiling. Paper lanterns, medieval music, platters of cheese and nuts and winter fruits on gold cloths.

'Come and meet some of my colleagues.' He'd taken barely a step when Yasmine, in a snowy Grecian-type robe that showed off plenty of bare shoulder, pounced on them.

Her sunburst headband of gold beads swayed as she pecked his cheek. 'Hi, there, handsome.' Then she linked arms with Ellie. 'Good choice,' she said, her charcoal eyes sweeping Ellie's costume. 'Come with me, there's someone I want you to meet and then we're going to check out what exciting treasures are on offer at the silent auction tonight. You don't mind, do you, Matt? John Elliot wants to talk to you about the zoning requirements for the Dockland development anyway.' She waved a vague hand towards the knot of men in the corner and swept Ellie away before he could mutter more than, 'No worries.'

He discovered he *did* mind. For once in his life he didn't want to talk business. He glared in Ellie's direction, watching her and Yaz disappear amongst a throng of women. He *wanted* to talk to his date. To share the evening with her, not with some hardnosed guy who never knew when to quit.

A bit like an older Matt McGregor.

The realisation was a solid punch to his gut. God, did he really see himself as a future J. H. Elliot? Middle-aged bachelor on the edge of a breakdown with nothing but work to fill his later years?

And wasn't that where Matt was headed? In less than twenty years he'd be alone on the wrong side of fifty too. Not so appealing.

But it could never be anything else. He, Matt, had engineered it that way.

He needed a drink to wash away the sobering prospect. He strode to the table, helped himself to a goblet of mulled wine, then mingled with staff as he manoeuvred his way to the windows where the lights of the city centre twinkled, and further out to the inky blankness of Port Phillip Bay.

'Matt.'

Distracted, he turned to see his receptionist wearing a heavily brocaded vermilion gown. 'Joanie. You're looking lovely tonight.'

'Thank you.' She handed him a squat fat candle. 'Looks like this solstice evening idea's a success.'

He nodded. 'How's the auction going?'

'Very well. What charity did you decide on?'

He'd thought of Ellie and knew she'd be happy with the idea. He'd already considered drawing up plans. 'We're going to give a local disadvantaged kids' homework centre a generous makeover. I'll give you the details later.'

Joanie nodded. 'A worthy cause.'

He spotted Ellie amongst the crowd talking with Spencer from accounting downstairs. Must be a fascinating conversation because she was smiling up at the guy. Leaning closer to hear what he said. Enjoying herself.

Which was what he'd wanted, right? But a fist knuckled beneath his breastbone and his jaw tightened as he watched them. He'd always disliked the guy.

'...so you know the tradition?' he heard Joanie say.

His eyes remained on Ellie. 'Yaz filled me in.'

'Why don't we make a start? I think everyone has a candle now.'

A tinkle of silver on glass got everyone's attention and at Joanie's request they formed a circle. Before the ritual got under way, Matt crossed the space and clasped Ellie's hand. 'Before we get started, I'd like to introduce Ellie.' He looked into those amazing eyes, felt himself falling, heard himself saying, 'She's with me.' Something inside him rocked off-centre; he'd never heard that possessive tone in his voice before.

But then a murmur of greetings followed, Yaz requested they seat themselves on the floor and the room was plunged into darkness. Only the city lights forty storeys below lent a soft sheen to the ceiling. It cast Ellie's face into dimness, but it was enough to make out her long eyelashes and the curve of her cheekbone. The tilt of her chin.

Vaguely he heard Yaz speak about long-ago traditions around the winter solstice. The battle between light and dark. A time for releasing personal resentments and regrets. He curled Ellie's fingers into his palm and his gaze remained locked on hers in the Moment of Silence for Personal Reflection.

Who was the real Ellie behind those violet eyes? Would he ever really know before he left? He knew some of her hopes, some of her fears. What of her secrets?

Her lips—a little wistful, a lot tempting. He bent his head to touch them to his. And lost himself in the warmth, her fragrance, her whisper of breath against his cheek...

Someone shuffled, Ellie drew back and he heard Yasmine's whisper at his other ear. 'Ah, Matt, when you're ready...'

He mentally shook himself. *For God's sake.* The sooner he left Melbourne, the better off he'd be. The sooner he could refocus on his work. His reason to get up in the morning. His life's core and purpose.

Rising, he placed his candle in the bowl of water which Yasmine had set in the centre of the circle. As he lit the wick, the tiny flicker glowed yellow against his palm. In turn, each participant stepped up, lit their candle from his, then placed it around Matt's. Finally Yasmine spoke of the Sun Child and the promise of light and a glowing future.

Lights were switched on, the music cranked up and goblets filled with all manner of spiced wines, ciders, beers. Caterers began bringing out platters of skewered meats and savouries. Hot herbed bread and appetising dips. A variety of soups served in chic individual shot glasses.

As Matt took Ellie's hand to lead her to the window, he noticed her bare arm. 'Where's your bracelet?'

Ellie didn't look at her wrist. She knew she didn't have the finances to contribute, so she'd done the only thing she could; she'd donated her bracelet to the cause.

'I haven't had the chance to tell you. When I learned you were donating the proceeds to the centre, I wanted to help. It's worth a lot more there than on my arm.' Before he could answer, she jumped in with, 'I'm sorry if that offends you.'

He tilted her chin up with a finger and looked steadily into her eyes. His touch was so infinitely gentle her stomach quivered. 'It doesn't offend me, Ellie.'

'I wouldn't expect you to understand, Matt,' she said softly. 'You wouldn't know about going without.'

For an instant she thought he was going to say something but then he shot her a curious look. 'If you'll excuse me a moment, there's a matter requiring my attention.' He did an abrupt about-turn and made his way through the hanging lanterns and across the room.

Turning away, she studied the panorama below. She *had* offended him. In this particular instance she didn't care. It was just another example of how they didn't fit as a couple, another reason to ignore her heart telling her this man was different. One of a kind. Special. She pressed a knuckle beneath her nose, telling herself the misty outlook was rain, not tears.

'Ellie? What are you doing here by yourself? Has Matt deserted you?'

She didn't need to turn to know it was Yasmine standing beside her, and just as well, because she didn't want anyone to see her infuriatingly damp eyes. Self-pity was not a good look. So perhaps her voice was a little too nonchalant, even acerbic, when she said, 'I'm just admiring the view. Amazing, isn't it? Matt's literally on top of the world.'

A brief silence. 'It took Matt years of sacrifice and effort and scaling Mount Everest to get here.' Yasmine sounded defensive.

Ellie's response was cool to her own ears. 'You two have known each other a while, then, I take it.'

'Twelve years. You're wondering about our relationship,' she said. 'Friends, confidants. Never lovers. Does that help?'

Ellie nodded, blurry eyes fixed on a skyscraper in the middle distance. 'I apologise if that came across as anything other than friendly curiosity.'

'Doesn't mean I don't care about him. If he was my brother, I couldn't care more.'

Ellie's gaze flicked to Yasmine's reflection in the glass. 'He's never told me about his family.'

'It's not something he talks about, with anyone. Not even me. But I do know he's achieved all this on his own. Worked his way through university, wouldn't take a cent from Belle.'

Her stomach suddenly twisting itself into knots, Ellie turned to Yasmine. 'Thank you for telling me. I think I just said something to him that I shouldn't have.'

Yasmine's smile was genuine. 'Why don't you go find him?'

Ellie stopped at the supper table with its sumptuous aromas and filled a plate, then looked about for Matt. She saw him on the far side of the room, one hand in a trouser pocket while he talked to a couple of guys and their partners. He'd removed his cloak and was in black from head to toe. He looked divine, if one could look divine and sinful at the same time.

Matt McGregor could.

He caught her staring and the hand in his pocket fisted, a muscle twitched in his jaw. His easy-going smile dropped away and his expression turned serious. He spoke to the group, then made his way towards her while her heart tried to find its rightful place in her chest.

Time seemed to slow. Everything but Matt blurred while he increased in clarity as he drew near. A hint of dark stubble on his jaw, the creases which didn't detract but rather carved his personality into his cheeks. Midnight eyes.

'Hungry?' she murmured belatedly when he reached her. Still looking at him, she lifted the delicious-smelling plate, noticing her hands were trembling slightly.

He plucked a snack from her offering. 'Yes. But I'm not thinking food.' He took a bite, slipped the other half between her lips, letting his fingers linger when she opened her mouth for the morsel.

She swallowed, still watching him. 'I did offend you. I'm sorry.'

'On the contrary,' he murmured back, holding her gaze. 'It was more of a reality check.'

'If I don't understand you it's because you haven't told me.'

But instead of an explanation, he took the plate, laid it on a nearby table, clasped her hand and said so that only she could hear, 'What say we get out of here?'

The raw and undeniable intent in his words, in his eyes,

shot sparks through her bloodstream. She let her sudden intake of breath out slowly. 'But don't you want to mingle?'

'I can think of better ways,' he replied, and tugged her out of the room and towards the bank of elevators.

Inside her apartment, he untied her cloak, laid it across a chair and slid his hands over her shoulders, up over her scalp and into her hair. 'I've been thinking about this all night,' he said, and kissed her. Slowly, deeply, deliciously.

But the tiny room was chilly, the old linoleum creaked and crackled beneath her feet. Yesterday's stale odour of fried cabbage from along the corridor permeated the air. A couple was arguing downstairs. 'My bed's too small for the both of us,' she whispered when he finally let her come up for air.

'We can make it work,' he murmured and kissed her once more, his hands cruising down her spine, over her bottom and up again.

Was this his attempt to show her he didn't care where she lived, who she was? It warmed her deep down to the centre of her being. 'But your bed would be much more comfortable….'

Lifting his head, he grinned, pulled out his phone and called back his driver. 'We've changed our minds.'

CHAPTER THIRTEEN

IN MATT'S room upstairs in Belle's house they were a world away from thin walls and peeling paint and noisy neighbours. The air was cool but not uncomfortable and tinged with the scent of his aftershave and fresh linen. A shaft of moonbeams slanted over the quilt. An owl 'mopoked' to another in the trees outside the window.

He undressed her slowly, skilfully, without the need for words. Her beautiful gown slid to the floor, her underwear followed. When she was naked but for her locket, he reached into his pocket and pulled out the string of sparkles. 'This is yours.' He clasped the stones, warm from his body, around her wrist. 'Please wear it, no questions asked.'

'But the auction wasn't finished when we left. You didn't *take* it, did you?' she said, momentarily horrified.

He grinned, kissed the tip of her nose. 'No, I didn't take it.'

'Then how—?'

He put a finger to her lips. 'I said no questions. All you need to know is that the money's going to a good cause.'

'Oh…yes.' Its elegant beauty and those deep dark eyes of his as they searched hers caught at her chest and made her nose sting and her eyes water. The way she saw it was he'd ensured his would be the highest bid before they left, and now she knew the money was to be donated, how could she refuse his gift for a second time? 'Thank you, it's beautiful,' she whispered.

'The centre's going to have those extensions you were talking about. I'll be there next week to take measurements and have plans drawn up.'

'Thank you doubly.'

But it wasn't the time to think of tomorrow or next week. That would come later, she thought—when she'd cry and berate herself for letting things get so complicated. For now, as he divested himself of his own clothes and watched her with a reflection of her own desires, she held the moment in her heart and rejoiced.

This moment of tenderness. Quiet murmurs and sighs. Gentle hands, soothing lips and a rolling, restless anticipation tempered by a patience that stemmed from the already familiar.

Moonlight carved a silver blade across his shoulders as he lifted her to the bed, laid her on the fine linen as if she was the most treasured of treasures. He stretched out beside her, and, oh…the feel of his hands as they skimmed over her body, every fingertip a glide of pleasure over shoulders, breasts, belly, thighs.

His lips now as they soothed the places his hands had delighted, warmth leaving a trail of moisture cooling on her flesh. He lingered over her breasts, teasing each nipple with tiny nips and tugs, then moved lower to curl his tongue around her bellybutton.

Slow, languid, yet she felt her breath being snatched from her lungs. Smooth as a glide of water, yet her pulse bumped and blipped as he shifted between her thighs and she realised his intent.

Lower. Skin sliding over skin. Spreading her thighs wider, he bent his head to bring her what she was afraid to want.

What some hazy part of her mind told her she'd remember on some cold and lonely day when he was gone. A memory.

And then even that was forgotten and she was soaring, flying apart into a million pieces, an explosion that shattered her awareness of self and the world as she knew it. He brought her down gently, with skill and a perception she'd never known he possessed.

And it came to her in that brief moment of stillness and fulfilment that, whether she willed it or not, this overflowing sensation of body, mind and spirit was indeed love. Freely given and without regret. Of feeling safe, protected, desired, and yearning to give it back threefold.

And yearning, yearning, to have it returned.

With his arms on either side of her hips, Matt looked down on her. Had he ever seen a more beautiful sight than Ellie rumpled with loving on his sheets? The warmth of her gold locket around her neck, the cool silver stones at her wrist, her halo of hair washed and bleached with the mystery of moonlight.

'You're almost too beautiful to touch,' he murmured, and saw her eyes fill with a poignancy that caught at his heart. He rolled on a condom, then bent to kiss those lush lips. 'Almost…'

Sliding into her slick wet heat was like coming in out of the cold. She took him inside her with a sigh, welcomed him with mouth and hands. She warmed places inside him he'd not acknowledged in…forever.

He moved inside her, in a slow sinuous dance, and she matched his rhythm as if she'd been made expressly for him. Here was sanctuary from the day-to-day demands in the cut-throat business world that was his life. In her arms that world didn't exist.

He was wrapped around her, she around him, and he felt

himself drowning, drowning, in the deepening well of her generous and open heart.

Still inside her, but sated and satisfied and blissfully lazy, they lay together in the darkness. Even as Ellie's breathing told him she was asleep, he didn't move, couldn't bear to complete the separation. He'd never known such a connection, a sense of completeness, of oneness.

Ellie was unlike anyone he'd ever known. She was proud yet vulnerable, with a strength of will and an empathy and generosity towards others. She wasn't pretending to be anything other than who she was.

Unlike him.

The sudden sharp chill of realisation sliced to his core like an icy blade. He hadn't been up-front about his past. Perhaps he should have. But it wasn't as if they had anything permanent.

And yet... As he watched her sleep, the curve of her cheek ivory in the dimness, he could no more deny he wanted her than fly to the moon. He wanted her more than his next breath. He needed her more than his next heartbeat.

But he knew all too well that desire, needs and wants wouldn't cut it with Ellie. He wasn't being fair to her. To them. With the spectres of lost loved ones haunting her past, if anyone needed love and constancy in their life it was Ellie. She'd tried so hard to hide it but he knew that, despite her assertions to the contrary, she wanted security, a home, family.

And he couldn't give her that.

Careful not to disturb her, he eased away. Already he mourned the loss of her sleepy warmth, the feel of her satin-soft skin against his. He stared up into the darkness.

Ellie... He sighed. Fiercely independent, living-life-as-it-comes Ellie. She wasn't as single, carefree and liberated as she let on. He knew by the shadows in her eyes when she thought he wasn't looking.

But over the past couple of days he'd seen glimpses of something else.... It twisted like a fist in his gut and clamped tight around the region of his heart. He'd seen something he should never have allowed to happen.

She was falling for him. The greedy, self-indulgent bastard that he was had seen it... Seen it and continued their affair with selfish and reckless abandon.

He needed to ride.

Slipping out of bed, he dressed quietly and went downstairs, grabbing his helmet and gloves by the back door, and strode out into the cold night air. He had to let her go. Tomorrow. Yes, she knew what they had was temporary—he'd always been up-front about that—but other emotions that he hadn't anticipated had entered into the mix.

His fist rapped the side of the helmet beneath his arm as he passed the garden, glittering with dew in the predawn. Ellie's garden. *'Dammit.'* His voice cut through the silent air like the crack of a whip. Knowing Ellie as he did now—the caring, vulnerable, love-starved girl that she was—he *should* have anticipated this could only end badly.

He wheeled the bike to the gate so as not to wake her, jammed on his helmet and fired up the machine the moment he was through the gate and set off for...who the hell knew? Cared? Anywhere out of town where the road was long and straight and relatively deserted at 5:00 a.m. Somehow he had to convince Ellie that he wasn't the right man for her.

Ellie tipped out another punnet of basil. As she'd drifted off to sleep she'd decided to get an early start this morning. To lie beside Matt, to feel the warmth of his hard masculine body all down her back, his slow breathing against her ear and wonder if it might be the last time was the best and worst of tortures.

But when she'd reached for him on waking she hadn't expected to find herself alone. She'd ignored the vaguely uneasy feeling at first, telling herself he was probably making coffee. But he was nowhere to be found.

Where was he and why hadn't he let her know his plans? He'd left no note, and when she'd checked the garage she'd discovered his bike gone. Perhaps this was something he did regularly, she comforted herself, like jogging; after all, she'd known him such a short time.

Yes, such a short time, she reflected, and despite all the self-talk and warning bells, she'd fallen in love.

She'd come outside hoping that working the garden would distract her from the dark and crazy thoughts buzzing around her head. She had plans today that she couldn't change. The job in Healesville was full-time but it was more than an hour away and involved catching buses and trains if she was going to stay in Melbourne. But it sounded challenging and exciting and she wanted to see what was involved. The appointment was for this afternoon.

She hoped Matt would be back before she left so that she could tell him—calmly, clearly—that she didn't appreciate his lack of courtesy because it had made her worry. That people who cared about each other or were in a relationship—*any* kind of relationship, no matter how temporary—were naturally concerned about the other.

Or was it already too late for all that? Was their relationship already over?

The full-throated rumble on the driveway heralded his imminent return. Setting her trowel on the muddy earth beside her, she watched his bike come to an untidy halt near the garage. He pulled off his helmet and gloves, set them on the ground. His expression was grim, from the compressed mouth to the shuttered eyes.

'Hi.' She stood slowly and walked towards him, dusting the dirt off her overalls while butterflies whirled crazily in her stomach. He didn't make a move to meet her midway, just stood there like one of Belle's crazy garden statues.

She stopped in front of him, those butterflies growing to monstrous proportions. His eyes were bloodshot, probably from lack of sleep but…she couldn't read them. He'd closed himself off from her. 'What's wrong?'

No response. Nothing. A mask of stone.

Then he reached out, curled his fingers around her upper arms. He smelled of leather and man. For an instant Ellie thought she saw remorse or regret or both. Then he hauled her to him, mashed his lips with hers. Heat, passion, anger—all that and more poured from his kiss in a surging tide that crashed over her, leaving her weak and shaken. Then he lifted his head, dropped his hands to his sides, took a step away—physically and emotionally.

She felt the distance like a chill wind sweeping through her soul and stared at him, not understanding. Rather, not wanting to understand. Because it was suddenly, devastatingly clear where this was headed. She steeled herself for it. 'Why are you angry?'

'I'm not angry, Ellie,' he said. 'Frustrated, perhaps. I'm flying back to Sydney today.'

It was delivered as a cool statement of intent. With no hint of regret on his part.

The big R.

He hadn't said it but it was clear as the prize crystal vase on Belle's dining table. She'd been rejected so often, left behind so many times, she should be immune to its effects now. Surely it wasn't possible for her heart to bleed any more than it already had? But she felt its life force seeping out, drop by drop.

Why? Their relationship had never been more than temporary. She'd always known, but it didn't make it any less painful. Gut wrenching. Heartbreaking. And yet…last night she could have sworn he…cared. Really cared. 'I thought you—' *we* '—had a few more days?'

'I'm needed there asap,' he said, his voice monotone. 'It's—'

'I know—business before pleasure.' She spoke over him, deliberately schooling her tremulous voice to somewhere approaching normal. It was time to reflect on the futility of it all and take control of her own life. Time to leave. This time it would be her doing the walking, not the other way round.

Somehow she pulled her numb lips into some sort of a smile. 'I understand. I really do. I've some business to attend to myself today. It's been good, Matt, but it's time to move on, we're not—'

'There you both are.' Belle's voice from the back door had them both turning. Still in her black overcoat, she walked towards them, her fawn hair riffling in the breeze.

'Belle.' Matt did an abrupt turnabout and strode to meet her, tension visible beneath his jacket's heavy leather shoulder pads. 'You should have let me know you were coming back today. I'd have picked you up.'

'No need.' She pecked his cheek, then looked past him, smiling at Ellie while she spoke. 'I thought you might be busy. I didn't want to disturb you so I caught a cab.'

From behind him, Ellie saw his shoulders lift. 'We were just—'

'Yes.' Belle smoothed his cheek, and even from where Ellie stood she could tell by Belle's expression that she'd seen them kissing.

And the rest…had she seen the rest? *Heard* the rest?

Ellie's legs were shaking so hard she thought she might have to sit down.

'I'll just let you two finish whatever you're doing and go and put the kettle on, shall I?'

'Be there in a minute, Belle.' He returned his attention to Ellie. Once more there was nothing in his blank expression when he said, 'Let's go and have that coffee with Belle. We'll talk about us later.'

No. There was no *us.* But she nodded and they walked to the house in silence.

Somehow Ellie managed to sit at the kitchen table with Matt and Belle and make conversation over coffee and chocolate biscuits, though what she said—what anyone said—she didn't remember.

But she did remember watching Belle. Slim black trousers, a hot-pink top with black lace edging. Her skin barely touched by her seventy-odd years. Short straight hair, blond barely streaked with grey and touched with gold highlights. Eyes that vacillated between blue and indigo…and something about the shape…almost familiar somehow… She'd never noticed that before.

Then she heard Belle say that she wanted to speak to Eloise on her own, 'For a little while, if you don't mind, Matthew?'

It wasn't a question and Matt knew it, had been expecting it even, because he rose, fingers stiff on the tabletop. 'Belle…I thought we were going to talk—'

'Thank you.' She smiled at him but her tone was firm. Final.

He left without a further word or a backward glance.

'We'll go into the lounge room,' she told Ellie. 'It's more comfortable.'

Belle chose an armchair and indicated that Ellie should

take one at an angle to hers. 'Eloise, when I went to my room I noticed you returned the angel. May I ask why?'

'My apartment was broken into the other night and I thought it would be safer back here.' Ellie's discomfort made itself known in her belly and she shifted uneasily on her chair. 'I love it, Belle, really, but I think it's more appropriate that you keep it. I'm only your gardener and Matt told me it's worth a lot of money.'

Belle acknowledged this with a nod. 'It is. I should have perhaps waited till now to give it to you, but I couldn't stop myself. Guardian angels are very important.'

'I don't understand.' Her voice quavered. It was such a valuable piece, why give it to Ellie? Her blood was pumping too fast around her body and she had a sudden urge to jump up and run as far away as she could. From Matt, from Belle. Except she was sure she'd fall into a dead faint before she reached the edge of the property. Worse, she didn't entirely know why.

'Eloise.' Belle leaned forward, her eyes seeking Ellie's. 'Your locket. Remember I asked you about it? You showed me the photo of your mother as a baby inside.'

Ellie's fingers rose automatically to the gold heart suspended around her neck on its fine gold chain. 'Yes...'

Belle smiled and it was the saddest smile Ellie had ever seen. 'I put that locket on my daughter the day she was born. The same day she was taken away from me.'

Ellie's fingers tightened on the metal and something inside her trembled. 'But Mum said...'

'It was 1963,' Belle continued, slower now, her eyes misting as she looked back to a time long gone. 'I was nineteen, unmarried and alone and I never saw my baby again.'

'Your baby...?' Ellie stuttered to a stop, the images colliding and coalescing like a watercolour painting in the rain.

'That baby was your mother. Eloise, I am your grandmother.'

CHAPTER FOURTEEN

'No.' ELLIE shook her head as much in denial as to try and make sense of it. 'My grandmother—Gran—died in an accident with Grandad and Mum when I was eight.' Twisting her locket in her fingers, she looked at Belle. The eyes...now she knew why they were familiar. *Because they were her mother's eyes.* 'How is that possible?' She heard her voice as if it came from somewhere outside her.

Belle reached out, took Ellie's hand in hers. 'You also have John's surname—Rose. Your grandfather and I were lovers. He was older but I had no idea he was married. I thought he loved me. Until I got pregnant. My parents disowned me, I had no one and I was desperate.

'John's wife, Nola—your gran—couldn't conceive, so he took the child on the condition that I never made contact. That I never saw my child again. Legally the baby belonged to him and Nola. I signed an agreement to that effect.'

'Oh, Belle,' she murmured, her eyes stinging as she imagined the pain of losing a child. 'How could he make you do that?'

'In those days there were very few options and I decided Samantha would have a better life with them than I could give her. John gave me this house as a form of payment.'

'But Mum knew this house belonged in her father's family.'

Belle smiled. 'Oh, I dare say John slipped up there at some stage. Or perhaps it was his pride. He was a wealthy man and my, oh my, he loved to flaunt it.'

Using it to tempt women like the pretty young Belle, Ellie thought, and hated her grandfather with a sudden and vehement passion. He'd cheated on Gran, stolen her grandmother from her and from her mother. 'You knew all this before you went away.'

Her smile faded. 'I did. When I saw your advertisement for gardening work in the paper, the surname leapt out at me, as it always does. But, Eloise…' She paused. 'Eloise was your grandfather's mother's name.'

'I know,' Ellie said. 'And I hate it. I only put it in that ad because I thought maybe it sounded more professional and would attract more clients. I'm not sure it worked.'

Belle smiled. 'It worked for me. You'd rather I call you Ellie?'

Ellie nodded. 'Please.'

'Then Ellie it is.' Belle folded her hands on her lap. 'But the name got me thinking. I did some research into his family history and made a startling discovery. I had no idea about the accident, or the fact that I had a granddaughter. Believe me, darling, if I'd only known years ago…'

'That's why you hired me? To get to know me?'

She nodded slowly. 'But after all these years…I wanted to decide whether I had the right to turn your life upside down. I went to see your grandfather's sister, Miriam, to talk it over with her, since she was one of the few people who knew the whole story.'

'Grandad never said he had siblings.'

'That's because Miriam never spoke to him again after what he did.' She took a deep slow breath. 'So, Ellie, I need to know…did I do the right thing? Your gran was probably a very important person in your life.'

'She was, but it was so long ago.' And now…now she had Belle. A miracle. And her whole being rejoiced. 'Yes, Belle, you did exactly the right thing.' She leaned forward and took both Belle's hands in hers. 'It'll take time to get used to the idea. I've been on my own so long. Matt will—'

Matt. Ellie's heart missed a beat. 'If Matt's your nephew and I'm your granddaughter…'

'Matthew's not my biological nephew.' She turned her hands over in Ellie's. 'He didn't tell you?'

'No.' She let a relieved breath out slowly. 'Closed book on that subject.'

Belle nodded but didn't elaborate. 'You two got close while I was away.'

She *had* seen them kissing. Ellie's eyes lowered to their joined hands and lingered there. 'Past history already.'

'Why?'

'For one, he lives in Sydney. And secondly, he's not the settling down, one-woman type.'

Belle was silent a moment. 'He's been working in Sydney for several months but his base is Melbourne, and where he works doesn't matter. As for the second…I need to know, what are your feelings for him, Ellie?'

Ellie bit her lip but tears sprang to her eyes anyway. 'He's the most…' She shook her head, unable to express the gamut of emotions he invoked in her—joy and love and pain and frustration. 'He'd do anything for you, Belle. I've learned that about him. He's loyal.'

'And once you've earned his loyalty you have it for ever, but you've not answered my question.'

Ellie's breath soughed out along with the emotions she'd just discovered. 'I love him—and, oh…I tried so hard not to.' She swiped her eyes and willed herself to toughen up. Take control. Smile. 'But I'll get over it.'

'Why would you want to?' Belle said softly.

'Because he doesn't want more than temporary.'

'If he gave that impression it's because he's been hurt before and worse, by people he loved that he should have been able to trust.'

'It wasn't an impression, Belle. He spelled it out loudly and clearly in capital letters and I was the fool who thought I was sophisticated enough to handle it.'

'I've never seen the look in Matt's eyes that I saw this morning when he looked at you,' Belle said.

Oh... If Ellie didn't get out of here right now she was going to blubber, so she stood, still watching Belle. *Her grandmother.* 'Matt. You... This is all so overwhelming. I want to stay and talk and ask questions. There are so many things I want to know, but I have to get home and change for an appointment at Healesville.'

Ellie explained about the employment prospect but reassured Belle she intended finishing the herb garden. That it was a good career opportunity but out of the city which was now not so appealing since they'd just found each other. Belle offered her the use of her car for the month if she took the job so that Ellie could remain in Melbourne with her.

They both rose and sealed the deal with a hug. A family hug of warmth and trust and welcome.

'I have to get the job first,' Ellie said, not wanting to end the embrace but finally pulling away. 'The bus leaves the city at one o'clock, which doesn't leave me much time.'

Belle squeezed Ellie's shoulder. 'Of course, darling. You do what you have to do.'

'But I can come back tonight and we'll talk some more...'

'Yes. Stay the night.'

Under the same roof as Matt? 'Oh, I—'

Belle hugged Ellie again before Ellie could say that wasn't going to happen, her grandmother's eyes glinting with purpose as she stepped back to look at her. 'I insist. And you'll come live here with me. However, I don't think Matthew has to know about any of this yet. But he and I do need to have a conversation.'

He should be packing. The aircraft would be ready for take-off at 2:00 p.m. Instead, swinging the spade, Matt vented his frustration on a patch of soursobs. He stopped a moment, scowled at the lounge room windows, but all he saw was the sky's reflection. No way of telling what was happening beyond those sparkling clean panes of glass.

The spade sliced through the soft earth. *Dig, lift, toss. Dig, lift, toss.* He concentrated on the fresh smell of soil-rich air, the repetitive sounds of his own grunts and the soft *plop* of mud building up beside him. Not allowing his mind to stray to a pair of soft eyes clouded with hurt.

Dig, lift, toss.

Throwing the spade aside, he swiped the sweat from his forehead, blew out a long laboured breath and stared back at the faceless window.

'Matthew. Are you digging your way to China?'

'Maybe I'm just digging my way into a big black hole,' he replied before turning. So focused on his own inner turmoil, he hadn't heard Belle approach. 'Is that what I'm doing, Belle?'

She folded her arms across her chest and looked him straight in the eye. 'I'd say that's highly likely.'

'Where's Ellie?' He was painfully aware that her name rasped up his throat like sandpaper and came out dry, scratchy. Parched.

'She left ten minutes ago.' Belle turned back and picked her way over the damp grass and towards the house. 'Come inside, we need to talk.'

* * *

'Talk to me about Ellie,' she said when they were seated in the lounge room.

He could still smell her sweet berry fragrance in the room. 'Not until I know what's going on, Belle. What did you talk to her about?'

'That's between me and Ellie for the moment.'

'I thought you—'

She held up a hand, the flash in her eyes daring him to continue. He shut his mouth. Belle was the only person who could cut him off with a look.

'I promised, I know,' she said, 'and I'll get to that. Right now I'm more interested in what's going on between the two of you.' She shook her head when he opened his mouth. 'And don't even think of denying it.'

Okay. Where to start? 'We…she…' He trailed off, unwilling, unable, to put his thoughts and feelings into words he wasn't sure he wanted to acknowledge to himself, let alone voice to another. 'Ah, Belle, since the age of ten, you're the one person I've always been able to come to for guidance and advice….'

'So what's changed?'

'This is different.' So different he'd never had to deal with anything remotely like it.

'There's something I've never told you, Matthew,' she said quietly. 'When I was nineteen, that man I told you about, the man I loved… We made a baby together.'

A baby… His gaze arrested on the woman who'd given him everything a child could want, and read the lingering sadness in her eyes. 'Belle…'

She shook her head and her eyes glinted with moisture. 'I listened to what others were telling me instead of my heart. I gave her up for adoption…and I've regretted it every day of my life since.'

Oh, Belle. Knowing Belle's gentle and loving nature, it

must have killed her to have been forced to do such a thing. He leaned out, caught her hands. 'I'm sorry.'

She tightened her fingers around his and looked deep into his eyes. 'What I'm trying to say here, Matthew, is that sometimes you have to make hard decisions, life-altering decisions, even when you don't have all the facts, knowledge or experience. Sometimes they're the right decisions, sometimes they're not. But you have to do what your inner voice tells you, not what others say is the right choice...or you may regret it the way I have.

'So, the question here is, what are *you* going to do about Ellie? If you love her, the decision will be easy.'

Love. Was that what this gut-wrenching pain and heartache and soul searching was all about? Love?

He didn't believe in love—not the foolish whimsical romantic kind. But he loved Belle. His love for her was rock-solid and abiding. He loved the honest, open, beautiful person she was both inside and out.

And when it came right down to it, wasn't that what he admired about Ellie? *Admit it, Matt.* It was *what he loved* about Ellie. The kind of love that wasn't going to fade. The kind that lasted for ever.

Without family support, Belle had made all her decisions by trusting her inner voice. Years ago she'd taken a chance on a kid called Matt with a murky background and a sullen attitude.

Now she expected the same of him. To take a chance, go with that gut feeling. He took a deep steadying breath to calm the hailstorm roiling within him. 'I take it you're not going to tell me why I've been here this past week as you promised you would.'

She shook her head. 'There's something you need to do first.'

Resigned, he acknowledged that.

'So I'll tell you only what you need to know. Ellie's leaving for Healesville this afternoon. The bus leaves at one o'clock.'

'Healesville? Why?'

But Belle only shook her head.

'Okay, go ahead and be stubborn.' There was no sting in his reply as he checked his watch. It didn't leave him much time. He kissed her on his way out. 'Thanks, Belle.'

The Southern Cross Station, a Mecca for travellers with its undulating steel roof floating above the vast cavernous space, usually fascinated Ellie. Today she didn't give it a second glance.

Her mind was still spinning with this morning's events. Belle. Matt. She felt as if she'd been forced through a meat mincer, dragged through a cyclone, then hurled onto a roller-coaster.

She presented her ticket and climbed aboard with moments to spare. The bus was crowded and already overly warm. She took a seat near the front beside a plump middle-aged woman who smelled of butterscotch. Ellie smiled at her then closed her eyes to forestall conversation. The engine's grumble vibrated through her bottom, passengers talked. The vent above her seat blew a refreshing draught over her face, letting her relax for the first time since she'd climbed out of bed.

It seemed like a lifetime ago. And in so many ways it was. Somehow she had to get her mind to focus on the afternoon ahead, if that was possible. For her own self-esteem as much as an income, she needed this job. She needed to get as far away from Matt as possible…except now she had a grandmother to consider.

Family.

Miracles did happen. A warm tide of emotion swamped her. She wanted to shout it to the world, to forget this job prospect and rush back to Belle. To throw her arms around her neck and tell her things she'd wanted to say to her mum all these lonely years, to tell her all about the daughter she'd given up.

Except her grandmother came with a nephew called Matt—who wasn't a nephew at all... That roller-coaster ride again.

She wanted to be near her grandmother, wanted to accept her offer to live there, and *damn it*, she *deserved* that. So how was it going to work because Matt would visit Belle and Ellie might be there and how was she ever going to get over him if that possibility was always lurking in the back of her mind?

'...need to speak with her.'

'...can't let you on without a ticket, sir.'

The familiar and impatient tone and commotion at the front of the bus had her pulse kicking up. Craning her head sideways she peered around the seat in front of her.

'I just need a minute.' Matt's voice rumbled over the sound of the engine.

His tall broad form blocked the entrance. His flattened hair stuck to his brow and he gripped the neck straps of a couple of bike helmets in one fist, brandished a bunch of dark windblown irises in the other.

Her heart swelled, then squeezed so tight she wondered that it didn't stop. Did he know irises meant faith and hope? How could he know they were her most favourite flowers in the whole world?

'Someone's about to get lucky,' murmured the woman beside her.

Then those dark eyes locked on Ellie's. Eyes that reminded her of storms and wild rides on motorbikes and all manner of risks. And pain. 'Don't be so sure,' Ellie murmured back. Just because she loved him didn't mean she was going to fall into those swirling depths because he willed it so. Definitely not. No way.

In two long quick strides he was towering over her and looking as confused—and determined—as she. 'Ellie. Please get off the bus. I want to talk to you.'

'No. And nor will I tolerate your stand-over tactics. Anything you have to say you can say here.'

If it were possible, his brow lowered further, and while passengers held a collective breath, she swore she heard the distant rumble of thunder.

He dropped the flowers onto her lap, then raked his free hand through his hair and lowered his voice. 'Come with me and let's sort this out.'

'There's nothing to sort out. You said it all this morning.'

His lips flattened, his white-knuckled hand gripped the seat in front of her. 'Is this you running off and being irresponsible again? Because I—'

'Excuse me?' She felt her vocal chords strain and stretch skyward. 'You were the one "running off" as I recall. To Sydney. As fast as you could.'

He acknowledged that with a barely-there shift in his posture, as if he had an itch between his shoulderblades he couldn't reach. Then, as if he was grasping at the last vine of summer, 'You can't leave—you haven't finished Belle's garden.'

'As of this morning that's no longer your concern.'

He leaned closer, his eyes dark windows to the roiling turmoil within. 'Another chance, Ellie.'

While her heart leapt at his words, a frown pulled at her brow. 'I'm confused. Are you giving me that next chance or asking for one?'

Hesitation. 'Both. Either. Whatever it takes.'

'And if I refuse…are you going to drag me off against my will like you did last time?'

A restless murmur of voices behind them. 'Not while I'm here.' The woman beside Ellie seemed to morph to monstrous proportions and placed a protective hand on Ellie's.

'Sir, buy a ticket or get off the bus.' She heard the driver's voice in the background.

'Damn it, Ellie... I...want you.'

The plea in his eyes almost undid her. But he'd brought this to a head this morning. Simple *want* was no longer anywhere near what she needed from Matt. She needed everything— total commitment, a lifetime, or nothing.

Either prospect terrified her.

She'd sworn never to surrender herself to another man again, yet trying to imagine a life without this particular man was a long, lonely road without end.

She looked away, down. At her hands twisting around the flower stems. Unless he offered her what she needed she had an appointment and she didn't intend to break it.

'Mate...*now*, or I'll have the transit police escort you off.' The driver's voice boomed down the aisle.

For two breathless seconds Matt stood his ground, then said, 'I'll be back.' His jacket creaked as he turned and made his way to the front of the bus, leaving the scent of leather wafting down the aisle behind him.

Ellie let her head loll back against the headrest and stared sightlessly at the seat in front of her. The sensation of numerous eyes boring into her transmitted a prickly heat up her neck.

'I'm Flo,' said her erstwhile protector, pulling a slim romance novel and cellophane packet from her bag. 'Persistent young man, isn't he?' She offered the packet. 'Butterscotch?'

Ellie shook her head. 'No, thanks. Not unless it comes without the butter.'

Flo chuckled. 'Men. Still, that one's got the looks. And

the potential, I suspect. I'd give it some thought if I was you.'
She unwrapped a sweet and popped it into her mouth before
opening her book.

One glance at the line-up snaking from the ticket office and
Matt knew he'd never make it. He turned back to see the bus
already reversing out of its bay. *Damn it all to hell.* Frustration
tied his belly up in knots as he jogged to the parking station
adjacent.

He was on his bike and into Melbourne's lunchtime traffic
and dodging trams along Spencer Street in less than three
minutes.

An hour later he cooled his boots while he waited for the bus
to pull in at Lilydale, the last stop before Healesville. He had
no idea whether Ellie was leaving town for good; Belle hadn't
exactly been forthcoming with information. Except he'd noticed
Ellie was dressed in smart black trousers and her jacket—not
what he'd have expected her to be wearing.

Either way, he wasn't going home without her.

He paced one way, then the other. It might be easier to walk
away from the best thing that had ever happened to him, easier
to deny what he felt than to lay his heart on the line. *To love.*
But Ellie... He gritted his teeth. Ellie made the whole risky
attempt worthwhile.

He was sweating up a lather inside his jacket as the bus
pulled up. His stomach took a dive as a few passengers disembarked, giving him sideways or lingering looks as they
passed.

When the last passenger had cleared the steps, he hauled
himself up and straight into the disbelieving gaze of the bus
driver. 'I know,' Matt muttered. 'Give a guy a chance.'

The driver shook his head, a half-grin on his lips. 'Okay,
mate. Thirty seconds.'

His heart jumped into his mouth when he saw Ellie's head poking into the aisle. Big dark eyes, the exact same shade as the irises on her lap. Porcelain cheeks. She was torturing her lower lip.

Ignoring the gaggle of onlookers, he fisted his hands at his sides to stop himself from going to her and dragging her off the bus and into his arms. Where she belonged.

Where she'd always belonged. His heart seemed to open up and swallow him whole. She'd belonged with him from the first time he'd seen her, he'd just been too blind to see it. Too damn stubborn to admit it, even to himself.

And now...was she leaving him? 'Ellie.'

She shook her head and implored, 'Get off the bus, Matt. *Please*.'

He wanted to tell her what was in his heart, right now, right here, in front of this busload of strangers, but he'd wait. There was something he had to explain first and it had to be done in private. 'I'll be waiting when the bus pulls in again, Ellie, and you *will* listen to what I have to say.' He meshed his gaze with hers, brief, blazing, intense. 'Think about that for the next twenty-five minutes.'

He nodded to the driver, his boots clattering on the metal step as he stepped off into the chilly wind.

From her position in the bus, Ellie couldn't see Matt as the vehicle pulled away, but a moment later she heard the roar of a motorbike and got a glimpse as he overtook them.

Her heart was jumping hurdles at a million miles an hour. Little chills were racing up and down her arms.

'I think he's serious,' Flo said around a mouthful of butterscotch, then sighed. 'Like Richard Gere in *Pretty Woman*.'

Oh, no, she'd had her share of *Pretty Woman*.

Flo resumed reading when Ellie didn't answer, too preoccupied with the way her world was spinning out of its orbit. For half her life she'd been afraid to open her heart for fear of the inevitable consequences, afraid to get close for fear of what *might* happen. But she wasn't the only one afraid today—for the first time she'd seen that same fear in Matt's eyes.

Belle had known her own share of fears and heartache but she'd worked through them. She thought of Belle's wise words of advice. Her grandmother loved them both. It was a starting point for new beginnings for the three of them.

She caressed the velvet petals on her lap with one finger and studied the rich purple shade and delicate yellow tongues. Hope and faith. Whether Matt knew the meaning of the iris or not, there was a message in there somewhere.

CHAPTER FIFTEEN

As THE bus rolled down Healesville's leafy main street and pulled into the depot, Ellie saw Matt's bike parked in front of the little shops next door and her heart picked up speed again.

The door opened with a hiss of compressed air. Passengers began disembarking. Ellie waited till most had left, then rose and let Flo pass by first.

It was a bit of a squeeze while the woman manoeuvred her wide girth out of the tight space. She gave Ellie a quick smile. 'Give that nice man a chance, now, won't you?'

Ellie replied with a vague, 'Uh-huh.' Finally, armed with her flowers, bag and business satchel hitched on her shoulder, Ellie made her way to the door. A few passengers lingered, waiting to be picked up. Or waiting for a final showdown? Ellie wondered, noticing a couple of discreet sidelong glances at her as she alighted onto the bitumen.

The wind whipped at her legs, her hair and the flowers she clutched. It also brought the aroma of onions and hamburgers from the shop nearby, reminding her she hadn't eaten lunch. Not that she could eat a thing what with her stomach twisting with all these nerves.

She saw Matt at the side of the bus, shoulders hunched, hands inside his jacket pockets. When he saw her, he picked up the helmets beside his booted feet and started towards her.

She watched him while her love wept from her heart. The emotion in his eyes was so naked, so raw, that she wanted to run to him and wrap her arms around him and never let go, but she stayed where she was.

A few hours ago he'd hurt her to the marrow in her bones.

When he was within arm's reach, he said, 'What are you doing here, Ellie?'

'Checking out a landscaping job.'

'A job.' His shoulders visibly relaxed, then he frowned. 'Way out here? You'll spend half the day travelling. I'll help you find you something in town.' Spoken as if the matter was already resolved. As if *everything* was resolved.

'No, Matt, *I* find me something, and right now I'm here to see if I like the look of this job and they like the look of me. It's only a four week contract.'

Matt judged the determined jut of Ellie's chin and decided that this was not the time to argue the point. 'Okay. Where is this job?'

'I have a map,' she said, hunting in her bag. 'I was informed it's only a ten-minute walk. This way.' She pointed down the Maroondah Highway. 'It's a bed and breakfast.'

'Maybe we can come here sometime and try it out, what do you say?'

'You're going back to Sydney,' she said, not looking at him. Not acknowledging the meaning he'd infused into those words *in any way*. She hugged her satchel and flowers as they turned off the main road and onto a quiet street bordered by winter grass.

'Only for a couple more weeks,' he said into the silence broken only by the wind. 'I'm not into long-distance relationships.'

She flicked him a brief sideways look, as if to say he wasn't into relationships of any kind.

And she'd be right. Barring the occasional fleeting acquaintance that lasted less than a few weeks, he hadn't had any meaningful kind of relationship with a woman in a long, long time.

But with Ellie it was different. It was right. With Ellie he wouldn't want it any other way. Yet looking at her now, every inch the professional in her business attire, hair tamed and sleek today, would she still be interested in what he had to say if she won this contract?

Or would she want to put all her time and effort into building a career? The way he had—until he'd discovered a career was no longer enough. The first night they'd met she'd told him she didn't want a family, that she loved being single. *Untrue.* Ellie craved love. But would she still insist she felt that way? After this morning, he couldn't blame her if she wanted nothing more between them. He had to convince her otherwise.

She checked her map, stopping in front of a little cottage. Primrose walls with china-blue trim. A large black pottery cat guarded the front door. Lichen-crusted stones overrun with ground cover flanked either side of the little path. No doubt about it, the garden needed attention, but Matt could see the potential. And the hours of work involved.

'Wait here,' she said at the gate and passed him the flowers. It squeaked on rusty hinges as she pushed it open. She walked up the path and he heard her speak to someone, then the door opened, closed.

A few moments later she reappeared with a middle-aged couple. They wandered the garden while Ellie made notes. Then he saw them shake hands. The couple went back inside and Ellie hurried up the path to meet him.

'I can't believe it.' She was breathless as he opened the gate for her. 'I start in two days. This is the biggest project I've worked on and they thought it would need two people but they're letting me do it on my own and if it takes longer they don't mind because—'

He put a finger on her lips. 'Ellie.'

'I'm rambling, aren't I? I can't help it. Today has been...' She trailed off and looked into the distance.

Matt saw his opportunity and took it. He pointed to an old wrought-iron seat by a clump of straggling bushes and headed for it. 'Let's sit down.'

Ellie's nerves did a double jolt. She knew she had to listen to whatever he wanted to say. But would what he said be enough? And what would her response be?

She walked with him, set her bags on the seat. 'I don't want to sit. Too nervous.' She rubbed her hands together in front of her face. 'I want to run....'

'Later. Ellie...' He stood too, with his heart in his eyes, the scent of warm leather and man wafting towards her. 'I don't know what's between you and Belle,' he said slowly. 'She wouldn't tell me. But it doesn't matter. You're what matters. You and me.'

His hands were cold as he reached out and cradled her face between his palms. His eyes searched hers, so deep it was as if he were looking into her soul. 'Is there a you and me, Ellie?'

There could be. If she was brave enough. Could she risk it? Could she take that chance? For however long it lasted— because last week he'd put a time frame on their relationship. Even here, now, he'd not mentioned anything permanent. And if he left, she'd never get over it. She'd never be whole, ever again.

And yet she had a grandmother who'd been through more than her share of heartache and loss. A woman of strength and courage and determination. And love. Love enough for both of them. For all of them.

What could Ellie be with those same genes flowing through her own veins?

Today Belle had shown her that she had a choice. Ellie could let love's hurts and disappointments twist her up inside and turn her into a bitter and lonely old woman. Or she could refuse that option and live in the light.

Matt saw the conflicting emotions behind her gaze and bent his head, brushed his lips over hers. A touch. A promise. Knowing, knowing deep in his bones, that it was a promise of for ever.

'I think I'll sit down now,' she said and collapsed onto the seat.

But rather than following her down, he remained standing and shrugged out of his jacket. The stiff breeze cut across his T-shirt, his nipples pebbled against the chill.

'What on earth are you doing? It's freezing.'

'Giving you the shirt off my back?' His half-grin faded and he gestured to the front of his T-shirt. 'Read it.'

His heart thundered beneath his ribs as she leaned forward. 'I didn't have paper with me,' he explained. 'It's a promissory note signing over half the house in Lorne to you.'

'I can read,' she said slowly, the colour dropping from her face. 'What I want to know is why?'

Squatting in front of her, he tugged her restless hands to his chest. 'Isn't it obvious?' He lifted her arms, kissed her wrists. 'Because I love you.' The words spilled from his lips as easy as water. Not so difficult, was it? Not when you meant it with all your heart.

He saw her jaw drop open. He saw that same love reflected back. But he saw pain there too, in those violet eyes, and he squeezed her hands. 'I shouldn't have left you the way I did last night, nor acted like a dumb-ass idiot this morning. But when Belle told me you'd gone, I knew I couldn't let you go.

'And before you say anything more, I've got something

else to say. I've not been honest with you and it's time I was. I want to tell you about Zena.'

'It's okay, you don't need to—'

'She was my mother, and I do need. She was the only family I had. The one person any kid should be able to count on. She was also Belle's housekeeper. She gave Belle one of the sob stories she was so good at and Belle, being the kind and trusting soul she is, gave us a room. One night she disappeared. Walked out on her own kid.'

He could remember it like it was yesterday. The bewilderment, the fear, the feeling that he wasn't good enough to love. The moody, unsociable kid it had turned him into.

'When she left, it was like a part of me shrivelled up and died. The part that trusted and let others in.' He closed his eyes briefly. 'Died, Ellie. I cut it out of me because I never wanted to risk feeling that kind of pain again.'

He felt Ellie's hands tighten in his but he didn't look at her. He looked at the tall thistle waving in the air beside his left boot. 'Luckily Belle took me in, but it took her countless hours of perseverance and dedication and unconditional love to break through to me. Eventually the courts granted her custody. We're not related but I love her and we're family.'

'That's what matters,' she said quietly. 'And that's what makes a family. The love.'

'I was in a long-term relationship only once. Her name was Angela and she wanted everything I couldn't give her. In the end it was she who left. And in many ways I was relieved to let her go.' He turned to look at Ellie then, searched her moist eyes and let his heart say the words. 'She wasn't the one I needed, the one I want. The one I love. You are.'

She gently tugged her hands from his grasp. 'Matt…I—'

'I know you said you didn't want a home and family. Neither did I. Until I met you. I want you to have a home you feel you belong in and I want to share it with you.' He kissed her chin, her brow. 'Because I want to marry you and spend the rest of my life with you.'

She was silent for so long, he didn't think she was going to answer and his heart dived to his boots.

Then she sighed. 'Ah, Matt...I want that too. I've been living scared. Every time I get close to someone I lose them, or they lose me.' Hugging her shoulders, she rocked back and forth on the seat, staring at the garden. 'Everyone I love always leaves. But you know what?' She turned her gaze to him, and light and determination shone in their depths, turning her beautiful face radiant. 'I'm through with living that way. I'm through being afraid of the past repeating itself, afraid to reach out and find happiness.'

'I promise you, Ellie, I'll never leave as long as there's breath in my body. And I want to put that promise in writing on a marriage certificate.' Grabbing her shoulders, he turned her to face him. His fingers tightened on her arms. 'I'll even let you eat the whole damn cheesecake whenever you want.'

The smile on her lips was the sweetest one he'd ever seen. 'The whole cheesecake, huh?'

'Every last crumb. Oh, Ellie, sweetheart, I love you so much.'

'I love you too, Matt McGregor. I love that you're loyal and kind and generous. You're honest and hardworking and care about people, and—'

He put a finger against her mouth. 'Right back at you, Ellie. And one day I want you to have my babies.'

'Babies?' Her eyes widened, darkened. 'You want babies?'

'Only with you. And when the time's right.' Then he kissed her. A long, lingering kiss that filled the empty spaces inside him with light and life and hope.

'I still want to work,' she said when he let her come up for air. 'It's important to me. At least, until those babies come.'

'You can work for as long as you want. I'll help you any way I can—study, business, whatever you decide. As a matter of fact, I need a landscaper to do something with my front yard.'

'A landscaper.' She grinned, her apple cheeks pink with the chill of winter and the warmth of happiness. 'I might be able to help you out there.'

He rose, tugging her up with him, hauling her close, and whispered, 'Let's go home and tell Belle.'

'Belle… Yes.' Ellie wound her arms around Matt's neck and kissed him again. 'And then she and I have some other news to share with you....'

EPILOGUE

Two months later

THE wedding was held in Belle's spacious home. Ellie wore a strapless cream gown shimmering with pearls, and a coronet of fresh spring flowers. She carried a bouquet she'd designed herself, a fragrant selection of freesias and irises tied with a wide purple ribbon.

Belle, in an ice-blue ensemble, gave Ellie away, and Yasmine, stunning in an emerald sheath, was her only bridesmaid. Yasmine's partner had flown in from Queensland the day before for the best man's duties.

Then Matt's colleagues and friends, now her friends too, shared the lavish buffet meal that followed.

No expense had been spared. Crystal and silver, caviar and champagne. And flowers—bowls of them on every available surface. A three-tiered cake towered in the centre of the room while a violinist, flautist and harpist performed one classical number after another.

'Mrs McGregor.' The voice behind Ellie was dark, sensual and husky as a large hand slipped around her waist.

She smiled and tilted her head to expose her neck. 'Yes, Mr McGregor?'

He nibbled at her earlobe, careful to avoid the new diamond stud earrings he'd presented her with yesterday. 'I have something for you.'

'Ah… Mmm, yes, so you do,' she murmured with a private grin. She could feel its hardness pressed intimately against her bottom. 'But it'll have to wait a while. We have guests and I don't think Belle would approve of us doing a disappearing act before the first dance, do you?'

'Probably not.' He chuckled. 'But that's not what I was referring to.' He turned her around and placed a tall cylinder in her hand. 'These are the final plans for the kid's centre's renovations. Work starts next week.'

'Oh, yes, yes, yes!' Holding it aloft, she did a quick pirouette. 'Thank you.' Her smile faded as she looked into his eyes and her love spilled over. 'Matt McGregor, you're the best husband in the whole world. And I love you. For ever.'

'For ever.'

Then he kissed her. Slowly, cleverly, meltingly…hot.

For ever.

Harlequin *Presents*

Coming Next Month

from **Harlequin Presents® EXTRA.** Available February 8, 2011.

#137 PROTECTED BY THE PRINCE
Annie West
The Weight of the Crown

#138 THE DISGRACED PRINCESS
Robyn Donald
The Weight of the Crown

#139 WHEN HE WAS BAD...
Anne Oliver
Maverick Millionaires

#140 REBEL WITH A CAUSE
Natalie Anderson
Maverick Millionaires

Coming Next Month

from **Harlequin Presents®.** Available February 22, 2011.

#2975 JEMIMA'S SECRET
Lynne Graham
Secretly Pregnant...Conveniently Wed!

#2976 OLIVIA AND THE BILLIONAIRE CATTLE KING
Margaret Way
The Balfour Brides

#2977 WIFE IN PUBLIC
Emma Darcy

#2978 THE UNDOING OF DE LUCA
Kate Hewitt

#2979 IN CHRISTOFIDES' KEEPING
Abby Green

#2980 KATRAKIS'S SWEET PRIZE
Caitlin Crews

REQUEST YOUR
FREE BOOKS!

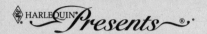 HARLEQUIN *Presents* ®

2 FREE NOVELS PLUS
2 FREE GIFTS!

YES! Please send me 2 FREE Harlequin Presents® novels and my 2 FREE gifts (gifts are worth about $10). After receiving them, if I don't wish to receive any more books, I can return the shipping statement marked "cancel." If I don't cancel, I will receive 6 brand-new novels every month and be billed just $4.05 per book in the U.S. or $4.74 per book in Canada. That's a saving of at least 15% off the cover price! It's quite a bargain! Shipping and handling is just 50¢ per book.* I understand that accepting the 2 free books and gifts places me under no obligation to buy anything. I can always return a shipment and cancel at any time. Even if I never buy another book, the two free books and gifts are mine to keep forever.

106/306 HDN E5M4

Name _____ (PLEASE PRINT) _____

Address _____ Apt. # _____

City _____ State/Prov. _____ Zip/Postal Code _____

Signature (if under 18, a parent or guardian must sign)

Mail to the **Harlequin Reader Service:**
IN U.S.A.: P.O. Box 1867, Buffalo, NY 14240-1867
IN CANADA: P.O. Box 609, Fort Erie, Ontario L2A 5X3

Not valid for current subscribers to Harlequin Presents books.

Are you a current subscriber to Harlequin Presents books and want to receive the larger-print edition? Call 1-800-873-8635 today!

* Terms and prices subject to change without notice. Prices do not include applicable taxes. N.Y. residents add applicable sales tax. Canadian residents will be charged applicable provincial taxes and GST. Offer not valid in Quebec. This offer is limited to one order per household. All orders subject to approval. Credit or debit balances in a customer's account(s) may be offset by any other outstanding balance owed by or to the customer. Please allow 4 to 6 weeks for delivery. Offer available while quantities last.

Your Privacy: Harlequin Books is committed to protecting your privacy. Our Privacy Policy is available online at www.eHarlequin.com or upon request from the Reader Service. From time to time we make our lists of customers available to reputable third parties who may have a product or service of interest to you. If you would prefer we not share your name and address, please check here. ☐

Help us get it right—We strive for accurate, respectful and relevant communications. To clarify or modify your communication preferences, visit us at www.ReaderService.com/consumerchoice.

HP10R

USA TODAY *bestselling author Lynne Graham*
is back with a thrilling new trilogy
SECRETLY PREGNANT, CONVENIENTLY WED

Three heroines must marry alpha males to keep
their dreams...but Alejandro, Angelo and Cesario
are not about to be tamed!

Book 1—JEMIMA'S SECRET
Available March 2011 from Harlequin Presents®.

JEMIMA yanked open a drawer in the sideboard to find Alfie's birth certificate. Her son was her husband's child. It was a question of telling the truth whether she liked it or not. She extended the certificate to Alejandro.

"This has to be nonsense," Alejandro asserted.

"Well, if you can find some other way of explaining how I managed to give birth by that date and Alfie not be yours, I'd like to hear it," Jemima challenged.

Alejandro glanced up, golden eyes bright as blades and as dangerous. "All this proves is that you must still have been pregnant when you walked out on our marriage. It does not automatically follow that the child is mine."

"'I know it doesn't suit you to hear this news now and I really didn't want to tell you. But I can't lie to you about it. Someday Alfie may want to look you up and get acquainted."

"If what you have just told me is the truth, if that little boy does prove to be mine, it was vindictive and extremely selfish of you to leave me in ignorance!"

Jemima paled. "When I left you, I had no idea that I was still pregnant."

"Two years is a long period of time, yet you made no attempt to inform me that I might be a father. I will want DNA tests to confirm your claim before I make any decision about what I want to do."

"Do as you like," she told him curtly. "*I* know who Alfie's father is and there has never been any doubt of his identity."

"I will make arrangements for the tests to be carried out and I will see you again when the result is available," Alejandro drawled with lashings of dark Spanish masculine reserve.

"I'll contact a solicitor and start the divorce," Jemima proffered in turn.

Alejandro's eyes narrowed in a piercing scrutiny that made her uncomfortable. "It would be foolish to do anything before we have that DNA result."

"I disagree," Jemima flashed back. "I should have applied for a divorce the minute I left you!"

Alejandro quirked an ebony brow. "And why didn't you?"

Jemima dealt him a fulminating glance but said nothing, merely moving past him to open her front door in a blunt invitation for him to leave.

"I'll be in touch," he delivered on the doorstep.

What is Alejandro's next move? Perhaps rekindling their marriage is the only solution! But will Jemima agree?

Find out in Lynne Graham's
exciting new romance
JEMIMA'S SECRET

Available March 2011
from Harlequin Presents®.

Copyright © 2011 by Lynne Graham

HPEXP0311

Start your Best Body today with these top 3 nutrition tips!

1. **SHOP THE PERIMETER OF THE GROCERY STORE:** The good stuff—fruits, veggies, lean proteins and dairy—always line the outer edges of the store. When you veer into the center aisles, you enter the temptation zone, where the unhealthy foods live.

2. **WATCH PORTION SIZES:** Most portion sizes in restaurants are nearly twice the size of a true serving and at home, it's easy to "clean your plate." Use these easy serving guidelines:
   - Protein: the palm of your hand
   - Grains or Fruit: a cup of your hand
   - Veggies: the palm of two open hands

3. **USE THE RAINBOW RULE FOR PRODUCE:** Your produce drawers should be filled with every color of fruits and vegetables. The greater the variety, the more vitamins and other nutrients you add to your diet.

Find these and many more helpful tips in

YOUR BEST BODY NOW
by
TOSCA RENO
WITH STACY BAKER

Bestselling Author of
THE EAT-CLEAN DIET®

Available wherever books are sold!

NTRSERIESFEB